THE VISCOUNT'S VOW

THE VISCOUNT'S VOW

JULIE COULTER BELLON

The Captain

The Capture

Second Look

Lincoln Love Stories

Love's Broken Road

Love's Journey Home

Copyright 2020 by Julie Coulter Bellon.

Published by Stone Hall Books

Cover Design by Steven Novak Illustrations

ISBN 13: 978-0-9997946-8-5

Printed in the United States of America

10 9 8 7 6 5 4 3 2 1

ACKNOWLEDGMENTS

I am so grateful to my family, friends, and fans who motivate me to write my stories and love them as much as I do. I couldn't do this without you! Thank you!

I also need to thank Jeni and Annette and my SWAT team who are the best support an author could have. They keep me going even with all my crazy deadlines. I appreciate them so much and wouldn't know what I would do without them.

But my biggest thanks is to my husband and family who give me time to write and always cheer me on. I love you and I'm so lucky to have you!

CHAPTER 1

*E*dward's pulse was racing. He could hear the pounding of the cannons, a staccato rumble that penetrated the fog surrounding his brain. He had to move. He had to find Marcus and get to a more secure location. Why couldn't he move? What the devil?

"My lord, open the door!"

The voice calling to him definitely wasn't his commanding officer, Christian Wolverton. It sounded like his butler, Jefferson. But what would he be doing on the battlefield?

Edward clenched his fists and tried to clear his head. He slowly became aware of soft carpet beneath his head. Where was he? Opening one eye, he saw an unlit fireplace in front of him. Not on a battlefield, then. The voice calling to him really was Jefferson. Coming fully awake, he remembered. He was at his townhouse in London.

"What is it, Jefferson?" His voice came out as little more than a croak. His mouth was dry and felt stuffed with linen. Swallowing, he tried again. "What is it!"

"I must speak to you. It is quite urgent." Jefferson sounded out of sorts. Much like Edward felt.

He rose from the floor and dusted himself off. Looking down, the shirt and breeches he wore were horribly wrinkled. His evening jacket and waistcoat had been discarded on the desk. He couldn't see his cravat anywhere. His valet would be vastly disappointed. Gibbs was a stickler for keeping Edward's wardrobe impeccably maintained and turning him out in the first stare of fashion.

Squinting his eyes against the sunlight that had managed to filter through the heavy brocade curtains, he tried to remember where he'd been last night. The Kensington ball. That's right. They'd had plenty of champagne and brandy in which Edward had freely indulged. He didn't remember coming home, though.

Rotating his shoulders to shake off the aches from sleeping on the floor, he opened the door, eyeing his butler. "What *is* it, Jefferson?"

Jefferson stared at him as if he were an otherworldly spirit come to haunt him. "My lord," he said, averting his eyes from Edward's unbuttoned and untucked shirt, not out of modesty, but to hide his disapproval. Jefferson was nothing if not proper.

Edward leaned against the doorjamb. He refused to ask for a fourth time. Instead, he would just wait for Jefferson to collect himself and state what the matter was. Besides, speaking made the ache in his head worse, and he'd decided on the spot to do as little of it as possible.

"My lord." Jefferson looked behind him, then leaned in. "Your *mother* has arrived. I put her in the drawing room, but she is most insistent that she have an audience with you immediately."

Edward groaned and his shoulders slumped against the wall. "Did you tell her I am indisposed?"

Jefferson bobbed his head. "Several times. She just marched past me and raised her eyebrows."

Closing his eyes momentarily, Edward pinched the bridge of his nose. His mother was barely five feet tall, but she had a commanding presence. "Fine. Tell her I'll be down directly."

Jefferson motioned to someone coming down the corridor, urging him to hurry. "I sent for Gibbs. And I also ordered a tea tray to be brought to your mother while she waits for you."

Gibbs scurried into view. He was a nervous man, but didn't ask questions and kept Edward's clothes pressed and ready. He could also tie a mathematical knot in a cravat. That was all Edward needed him to do.

Gibbs bowed. "I brought you a posset from Cook, my lord. It should help your head." He handed Edward the cup and a horrible smell hit Edward the moment it was in his hand.

He reared back. "What the deuce is in this?"

"Cook's secret family recipe, guaranteed to cure a sore head." Gibbs carefully stepped around Edward and walked toward the wardrobe. "What would you like to wear to greet your mother?"

"I won't be changing." Edward peered into the murky brown liquid of the posset. Did he dare drink it? He could just make out some suspicious-looking lumps floating on the side.

Gibbs turned to face him, his face aghast. He pointed at Edward's attire. "But, my lord, your mother couldn't possibly be expected to receive you in . . . in . . ."

Edward held his breath and tossed back the drink as quickly as he could. It tasted as disgusting as it looked. He swallowed again so he wouldn't cast up his accounts on Gibbs's boots. "My mother is not receiving me. I am receiving her. And as she has arrived unannounced, she'll have to take me as I am."

He handed the gaping Gibbs his empty cup and strode out into the hallway. As a sort of compromise, Edward did manage to run his fingers through his hair and tuck in his shirt. He hadn't lost the entirety of his manners after all. Reaching the door of the drawing room, he hesitated to open it. There was only one reason for her to come to London. One he didn't want to discuss.

Ever.

If he didn't receive her, though, his mother would search the house for him. She was not one to be put off. With a sigh, he opened the door.

She was sitting in the high-backed chair near the fireplace, her pale hands in her lap contrasting with the severe black of her mourning gown---a reminder that he should also be wearing at least a black armband for his own mourning attire. The thought made his head pound again.

At his entrance, she stood, and even the whisper of her bombazine gown swishing around her feet seemed loud. With a quick glance at his apparel, his mother's mouth pursed into a tight line. "Edward."

It never failed to surprise him how she could make his name sound like an admonishment. "Mother, what a surprise."

She raised both brows and waved toward his attire. "I can see that."

He slowly walked to where she stood, gritting his teeth at the pain in his head made worse by the overly bright room. Who had opened the curtains at this time of morning? "Could this not have waited until evening?"

Though he wasn't planning to be at home then. He anticipated finding another ball or musicale where alcohol flowed freely and there were enough people to divert him from the otherwise empty hours stretching eternally in front of him. Too much time to think. And remember.

The viscountess sat with a heavy sigh, and Edward gratefully sank into the chair next to hers. Blinking, he stared at her disapproving face, then turned away.

"I can't let this nonsense go on any longer," she said softly, leaning over and taking his hand in hers. "I should have come to you weeks ago. Perhaps I could have saved us both some heartache."

"Father wouldn't have wanted that." Edward shifted uncomfortably in his seat. He'd need something to drink if the conversation went much further.

"He wanted exactly that. Didn't you get his messages?" His mother's other hand came over to rest on top of his, sandwiching his fingers between hers.

"I got them. But I assumed he was calling me home only to once again remind me of my station, my duties, and my responsibilities." How was he to know his father had truly been on his deathbed? He'd thought it another ruse to lure him home, but now he'd missed the only chance he would ever have to reconcile with his father---all because of his own pride.

His mother patted his hand as if he were once again a small boy. "He had so much he wanted to say to you."

Edward pulled his fingers away, her touch adding fire to her reprimand. "Yes, I know I've disappointed you both." He pushed a hand through his hair. "But then, I was always a disappointment to Father."

His mother pressed back into her chair with a long sigh, releasing his hand. "You and your father had difficulties, but he always loved you."

Edward wanted to shake his head. His father had loved the idea of molding a son into someone who cared only for performing their duty and responsibility. There had never been room for Edward's own ideas on what his life should be. "Did you come to discuss Father?"

The door opened, and his mother paused while the maid brought in a tea service. She set it all out on the table next to the viscountess and bobbed a curtsy before she left. When the door was once again shut, his mother poured a cup of tea for him, with two sugars and a dollop of cream, just how he liked it. With the way his stomach was roiling, however, he didn't know if he could drink it. He took it anyway.

She stared at him over the rim of her cup. "I came to ask you to come home to Hartwell Manor," she said before she took a sip.

He couldn't do it. He couldn't go back there. "No."

She set her saucer back on the tea tray and faced him, unfazed by his flat refusal. "It's time, my son. It's been too long, and you're the viscount now. Like it or not, you have responsibilities and duties that must be tended to."

How many times had his father said the same thing? That he had duties and responsibilities. That he was *born* with duties and responsibilities. Edward stared into the fire, letting her words wash over him. He never wanted to be in this position---to be the viscount. That was partly why he'd run away and joined the army. "The steward is doing a wonderful job. I get weekly reports. There is no reason for me to be present."

"It's time to come home. The estate needs you. *I* need you." His mother's voice was soft, yet firm.

He looked over at her with a frown, fear twisting through him. "Are you in ill health, too? Is that why you're so insistent?"

She held up a hand in reassurance. "No, no, I'm quite healthy, and God-willing, will stay that way. But you've been home from the war for months. I'd like to get to know you again."

There was pleading in her eyes, and Edward groaned inwardly. How could he refuse his mother? So many men on the battlefield had called for their mothers at the end, wanting to see them one more time. He'd survived and had another chance to be in his mother's company. He wouldn't waste it, though he'd rather have more time to control the night terrors he'd been experiencing since he'd arrived back in England.

"Very well, Mother. I can come to Hartwell for a few days." He clenched his teeth. He could likely manage a short visit and be back in London before the next round of entertainments later in the week.

The viscountess immediately shook her head. "I'd like you to have an extended stay. You were gone for two years. Surely you can find it in your heart to visit with your mother for a month or two." She shifted in her chair and twisted her fingers in her lap. Edward suddenly realized that she was nervous to ask him to come home.

He knew what his duty was regarding the estate and his mother. If nothing else, his father had lectured him on that topic from the time he could walk. With a sigh, he looked at his mother's face. She was still beautiful, but there were shadows under her eyes and lines around her mouth that hadn't been there when he left for war. Perhaps it was time to go home, then. "Of course. I'll pack for an extended stay."

She clapped her hands and stood with her arms outstretched. "I'm so pleased. And I know Charlotte will be as well. She's faithfully waited for you."

Edward stood and obediently went into his mother's embrace, but his mind was on the woman who'd faithfully waited. Even just hearing her name caused his chest to constrict.

Charlotte.

Long hair, the same beautiful color of a good Spanish coffee, teasing eyes, and a ready smile. The only woman he'd ever loved and the one he was trying to forget.

He clenched his jaw, pushing the memory away. "I'm sure

Charlotte won't be pleased to see me when David informs her that our betrothal has been broken."

His mother pulled back, her eyes wide with surprise. She put her fingers to her mouth and shook her head. "No! Edward, you wouldn't do that to her. She loves you."

"It's nearly a *fait accompli*." He grimaced. "Another disappointment to add to your collection regarding my actions." He stepped back and clasped his hands in front of him. "I'll present myself at Hartwell tomorrow, Mother. But you may regret your invitation."

He didn't wait for his mother's reply, just gave her a stiff bow before walking out. Truth be told, he didn't want to see any agreement in his mother's eyes that he truly was a disappointment to her or that she might regret her invitation. No, the only thing he wanted to see right now was his bed.

And maybe the bottom of his glass so he could forget what his life had become.

CHAPTER 2

*C*harlotte dismounted from her favorite horse, Samson, and handed the reins to the groom. She was exhilarated after her ride. The mist had burned off the park and the chill in the air was invigorating. It was a beautiful morning, made all the more so by the news that Edward was returning home today.

Her heart skipped at the thought of finally seeing him after all this time. Two years, eight months, and sixteen days. She held her hand to her chest. Their last meeting had been full of fervent promises and declarations of love. She'd kissed him ardently under their tree, and she'd not regretted it. Instead, for the last two years, she'd relived every moment of his lips touching hers and his hands pressing her so close. It had felt as forbidden as his flight to join the army. They knew his father would be furious, but leaving seemed to be the only way to escape the viscount's iron grip and his endless lectures on Edward's responsibilities and duty.

I am going to be my own man, Edward had declared. Then he'd taken her fingers in his own and vowed to meet her again in that very spot when he returned home from war. Then they would marry and dance the waltz at their wedding ball.

Charlotte smiled as she walked down the path to Winslow Hall. She loved her country home. It had always been a refuge and her best memories of Edward were here. She could hardly wait to see him. Did he plan to meet her under their tree in the wood, as he'd promised? Would it be folly to go to Hartwell this afternoon and wait? She couldn't decide.

As she ascended the steps to the house, Livingston, their butler, opened the door. "Good morning to you, my lady. Did you enjoy your ride?"

"I did at that." She unpinned her hat and took off her gloves. "Do I have any messages?"

Livingston nodded as he held out a hand to take her things. "The vicar sent round a note. Mrs. Atherton has had her baby. Another fine son."

Charlotte's mouth dropped open in surprise. "I was so sure this one would be a girl. Eight sons," she marveled. "Mrs. Atherton will need a larger garden to keep them all fed."

The butler stood there with a small smile playing around his lips. "Yes, my lady."

"Well, I'll send a basket 'round, then go visit her in a few days. Anything else?" She was a bundle of nervous energy and wanted to go upstairs to change out of her riding habit and choose the gown she'd wear to see her betrothed. She'd been waiting so long for this day and didn't want to waste a moment of it.

"Your brother is in the library and has requested to see you." The butler looked down the hallway, where the library was located, then back at her. "The earl seemed most anxious."

Well, anxiety was never a word she would use to describe David. She'd best go see what he wanted right away. "Thank you, Livingston."

Charlotte strode down the hall. What could David be anxious about? Had he seen Edward in Town? Had something happened to him? No. After two years, surely fate wouldn't play such a cruel trick. Her steps quickened.

She nearly burst into the library. David was impeccably dressed in a blue morning coat and tan breeches as he paced in front of the fireplace. He looked up sharply when she entered. "You look like the devil is chasing you," he said, raising his brows. "Are you well?"

"Quite well." Charlotte moved into the room, walking to him and taking his hand. "Livingston said you wanted to see me and looked particularly anxious. Has something happened?"

David let out a breath and avoided her eyes, instead staring at the door, as if he'd rather take his leave than speak with her. "Perhaps we should sit."

Charlotte didn't budge. A tremor of fear went through her that David was sure to have noticed. She pulled her hand away from his grasp. "Something *has* happened. Tell me at once."

He arched a brow, and Charlotte let out an exasperated puff of air. Taking two steps to the nearest settee, she sat down and looked up at him. "Please tell me."

David sat beside her and gently took her hand in his. "I wish I had better tidings because the news I have is such that I'm dreading to tell you."

Charlotte's heart sank to her toes. "Is it about Edward?" Her voice was little more than a croak. *Please don't let him have returned home from war only to be hurt here at home.*

"In a roundabout way, I suppose it is." David sat back and ran his hand through his hair, mussing the Brutus style his valet must have spent time combing just right this morning. "Since he's returned to England, he's a changed man, Charlie. And not in a good way."

Charlotte frowned. "What do you mean?"

"He is nearly always foxed. He seems to care nothing for his reputation and has been frequenting gaming clubs that no respectable gentleman would enter." David looked down at her. "And engaging in behavior unfit for a lady's ears."

"That's ridiculous. I'm not a green girl. Just tell me what you mean to say." Charlotte pursed her lips, her mind racing with all the actions society could hold against Edward. Had he not paid a gambling debt? Or perhaps he'd slurped his soup in company? The rules of the *ton* were sometimes silly, but absolute, and anyone could be censured whether they committed the *faux pas* or not. "This is my betrothed we speak of, David. I must be informed if something is wrong."

David cursed, and Charlotte lifted her eyes to the heavens. Older brothers could be such a trial. "Was that fit for a lady's ears?" she said with mock-exasperation, trying to lighten the heaviness of the moment and calm her own anxiety.

"I apologize, but this is so deuced hard to say." David stood and began to pace again. "When father died, the Pembroke estate was in dire straits. I did my best to settle the debts, but a few remained outstanding. I made a bad investment, but had a streak of luck at the gaming tables and thought I'd found an easy way out of our predicament, but I lost. The little money I had set aside for estate repairs and such was gone." He looked over at her, his eyes haunted. "I couldn't tell you or Mother. And then when I was accused of murder, the debts were called in, and I couldn't pay them."

Charlotte could hardly believe his words. Their family had been through this very thing with their father and the estate and all the people it supported had suffered.

She put a hand to her middle, a sick feeling coiling through her. "Oh, David. You gambled it all away? Is there any left?" Her voice trembled, though she did her best to keep it steady.

The look of devastation on his face was answer enough. "I was sure I could fathom a way out of this fix before things got out of hand and those who were owed money came calling. I was going to marry Lady Alice and use her dowry, but that plan went awry when she fell in love with someone else. By then, the creditors were becoming most insistent. I was nearly reduced to hiding in my apartments without so much as a visit to my club, but, by some miracle, they suddenly stopped calling. The debt had been paid." David returned to his seat and put his hand over hers. Exhaling, he met her gaze. "Edward had bought up all my vowels."

Charlotte smiled, her anxiety melting away as her heart warmed with the words. Edward had saved them. He'd always had such a giving nature. "That's wonderful! Of course he would help you out of a fix. You were boyhood friends. It only makes sense. Besides, you're going to be family to him soon."

David squeezed her fingers, pity in his eyes as he stared at her. "Edward didn't buy them as my friend, Charlie. He bought them as leverage."

Her brother spoke slowly, but Charlotte's brow still furrowed in confusion. Nothing about this conversation was making sense. "Leverage? Whyever would he need leverage over you?"

Every muscle in David's body seemed to tense, and Charlotte felt a deep sort of foreboding that the words he spoke next would change her life forever. Yet, there was nothing she could do to prepare. She kept her gaze steady. "Just say it."

"We won't be family, Charlotte. If you don't break the betrothal with Edward and cry off, he will ruin us. And since he holds all the debt the Pembroke estate has, it's not an empty promise." His jaw clenched. "I'm so sorry. This is all my fault."

David's words hung heavy in the air as she tried to make sense of them. Charlotte blinked, and all the breath in her lungs seemed to rush out of her. She couldn't have heard him correctly. "Edward wants me to cry off and is threatening you if I don't?"

David squeezed her fingers again, as if her hands were about to break into pieces and he was singlehandedly holding them together. "I'm sorry, Charlie. So blasted sorry. But if you could have seen him and his actions around Town lately, you would *want* to cry off. He's not fit to be your husband anymore."

Charlotte pulled away and stood, turning from David and his eyes full of pity. She could hardly breathe. Putting her hand to her head, she tried to organize her thoughts. Edward didn't want her for his wife? That didn't make sense. They'd been planning to be married since they were old enough to notice each other. He'd vowed to come back for her, to take her away. What had changed?

"You must be mistaken." Her voice sounded hollow. Swallowing, she turned back to David. "There's been a misunderstanding."

David stood and put his hand on her shoulder. "His solicitor has already set out the terms in writing. We must give our response and signature by the end of the week." His voice was so soft she could barely hear him over the roaring in her ears.

Tears spilled over Charlotte's cheeks. She swiped them away. "I won't agree to anything until I speak to Edward."

"He won't see you. That's one of the stipulations. You must stay away." David moved to face her. "As I said before, he's changed. He's not the man you knew and loved. He loves nothing but champagne and frivolity now."

Even as David spoke, Charlotte couldn't imagine Edward like that. She couldn't remember a time in her life without her steady, sweet Edward. He'd been her best friend, her first kiss, and her only love. No, this was all wrong.

Edward was meant to be hers, and she was going to hold him to his promises. "I must speak with Edward. Immediately." That was it. She'd speak to him and straighten this all out. David had misunderstood something. That was the only way any of this made sense.

She walked out of the library without another word and climbed the stairs. This misunderstanding would likely prevent Edward from meeting her at their tree like they'd always planned. Her heart cracked a little. Today was supposed to be the happy homecoming she'd dreamed of, and now it would be full of wondering how soon she could speak to Edward alone and straighten out the confusion between them.

Charlotte continued on to her bedchamber, her thoughts racing. What if what David had said was true? If it was, she did know one thing.

Edward wasn't going to get rid of her that easily.

CHAPTER 3

The sound of the door crashing open reverberated through Edward's head with such pain that he could barely bite back his groan. His eyes were gritty and stuck together so tightly that he could hardly open them.

"Edward James Rupert Rutledge."

Oh no. Mother had used his full given name. He managed to open one eye to see his mother standing over him, her hands on her hips.

"Did you sleep all night in your father's study?" She touched the empty snifter of brandy next to the ink blotter on the desk, then brushed her fingers off as if the snifter were dirty.

"As the new Viscount Carlisle, I believe this is *my* study." Edward sat up with a muffled groan. If this had still been his father's study, he wouldn't have been lying down or even sitting in it. The only reason he would have been there was to stand in front of the desk and receive a lecture.

From an early age Edward had heard his father articulate on many occasions that he needed to be more responsible and look to his duties. Edward could very nearly predict what his father's next words would be during their interviews. He would be admonished to do more. Be better. But at least holding his hand out for a cane lashing had stopped when Edward had finally grown taller than his father. He hated this room.

"Yes, yes, of course it's your study." His mother's brows drew together as she stared at the now-empty study walls. "What did you do with all the paintings?"

"I had the staff take them to the attics." His father had hung a monstrous portrait of himself over the desk. That one had been the first to go. His grandfather's had been next. All of the portraits that his father had loved were far away from Edward's sight. He planned to do the same with every chamber and hall in Hartwell. Maybe he couldn't erase what he'd endured here, but he could make sure those experiences didn't haunt him every time he walked into a room. He had enough ghosts to deal with already.

His mother took a breath and peered down at him, apparently deciding not to say anything more about the empty walls. "I only came to inform you that it's nearly time for church." The look on her face was one Edward remembered well from boyhood. He wanted to stand and say, *Yes, Mother*, immediately. But he couldn't. Not this time.

"I won't be attending services today, I'm afraid." His head was pounding and the thought of hearing the vicar expound on the damnation of men's souls made it ache even more. After what had happened on the battlefields of Spain, Edward's soul was bound for hell, but he didn't want to listen to all the reasons why he wasn't fit to sit in church with the good townspeople.

"Nonsense. The Rutledge family never misses church." His mother turned to a maid standing behind her. The viscountess held out her hand for a glass of dark liquid and handed it to Edward. He reluctantly took it. "Your valet gave us the recipe for the posset you normally drink in the morning, and I had Cook make it up for you. The carriage will be ready in a quarter hour."

With one last glance that told him all her expectations with just a look, she took a deep breath and quit the room. Her black skirts swirled around her like a storm cloud, matching the expression on her face.

She was a formidable woman and was obviously disappointed in him. Again. Edward massaged his temples. No matter what he did, he let people down. His father. Marcus. Now his mother. He couldn't do much for Marcus or his father, but he had to at least try to please his mother. She'd stood by him faithfully, no matter what. He owed her his best efforts. Quickly drinking the putrid-smelling liquid in the glass that tasted a bit like rotten cabbage, he set it on the tray.

He was going to church. For his mother.

Feeling somewhat unsteady, he made his way to his bedchamber. Gibbs nodded when he entered and moved toward the bed, where his best jacket and breeches were laid out. Edward grimaced. He'd rather join his clothing on the bed than dress for church, but he straightened his spine and quickly washed and dressed without a word. The valet seemed to sense the need for silence and didn't attempt a conversation. At a quarter past the hour, Edward was striding downstairs just as the carriage arrived out front.

When she saw him, his mother's eyes gleamed with approval. He offered his arm and she tucked her hand into his elbow as they slowly made their way to the waiting carriage. "Thank you," his mother said softly as he handed her in.

He'd done something right and her face held no trace of disappointment. The band that had been squeezing his lungs loosened a bit. Allowing himself a small smile, he joined her inside the carriage and it started down the drive. The church wasn't far, but the weather was turning chilly and the carriage would offer some protection from the elements.

Edward looked out the window. The trees had lost their leaves. It was nearly winter, and somehow he felt like he'd only just returned home. Yet, he'd come back to England in the spring. Summer and most of autumn were a blur for him. He shifted uncomfortably in his seat. His method of suppressing the nightmares had worked, but he didn't like the feeling of not clearly recalling his actions these past months.

They arrived at the church, and when the steps had been set, Edward got out first, then reached back to help his mother.

"The vicar will be so glad to see you," his mother said as they started toward the steps of the church. "He prayed for your safe return. We all did."

But Edward hardly heard his mother's words. There was a woman already greeting the vicar at the doorway.

Charlotte.

She was so beautiful. Her brown hair still had reddish highlights in the rays of sunshine that poked through the clouds. She had been a ray of sunshine for him once. He'd felt like he couldn't breathe unless she was near. And that feeling persisted. The closer they got to the doorway, the less he could breathe. Should he get back into the carriage? But his mother pulled him along.

His steps slowed, and he felt his mother's gaze, but all Edward could see was Charlotte. She gave the vicar her bright, wide smile, and Edward's heart nearly stopped. He'd once lived to put that smile on her face. Since she hadn't yet noticed him, Edward took the time to look closely at her. She wasn't the girl he'd left two years ago. Her face was more angular, her curves filled out into a womanly shape that any man could appreciate. Before that last battle, he'd imagined this moment of seeing her again so many times. Pulling her to him. Kissing her. The need to hold her was almost an ache. It had been so long. Edward clenched his hands.

They drew near to the vicar and Edward felt as if a vise were squeezing his lungs. Charlotte turned to him and smiled, the same smile he'd always loved. Her eyes had a shadow of sadness in them, though, and his joy at seeing her wilted. Her brother must have told her of his demands to break their betrothal. He hated that he'd hurt her, but someday she would thank him. It was for the best.

He stiffened his spine and inclined his head. "Lady Charlotte. Vicar."

Charlotte's smile faded at his formal tone. She dipped her head and curtsied. "Viscount Carlisle."

The title sounded foreign coming from her. He'd always been her Edward. This was wrong. All wrong.

His mother made her greetings and they moved inside, leaving Charlotte and the vicar in the vestibule. The church was centuries old and the familiar, musty smell washed over him, rather like an old friend welcoming him back. His boots were loud on the stone floor as he made his way down the aisle. The villagers already seated on the benches all craned their necks to stare, some nodding in greeting. He knew most of them from his boyhood, and they'd aged and changed just as he had.

He stiffly walked to the family bench and helped his mother sit before he joined her. He took his regular seat on his mother's right, leaving his father's seat to her left empty. It would have seemed strange to sit where his father had. Though Edward was the new Viscount Carlisle, he wasn't merely replacing the old one and he didn't intend to walk the path his father had set.

Whispers erupted around them, but he ignored all of it and stared straight ahead. Were they whispering about his return? His father's recent passing? He was sure he didn't want to know. The Pembroke bench was directly behind the Carlisle one, and he could feel Charlotte's presence when she took her seat. Edward resisted the urge to turn around. To talk with her. He had to stay strong. Let her go.

Closing his eyes, he concentrated on breathing. The pain in his head had increased, and he wished to be at home in his bed. Preferably with a snifter of brandy to shut out all his feelings.

Mercifully the vicar walked to the front and began his sermon. His chosen topic was forgiveness, something Edward knew he'd never be able to find. The men he needed to beg forgiveness from were all dead. He bent his head. Their faces went through his mind. Marcus. Steven. Alistair. Men who'd had a whole future ahead of them, but whose lives had been cut short. He should have done more. Saved them.

His thoughts crowded in until his heart began to beat like the wings of a wounded bird. He tried to find something else to look at, to think about. The diamond-shaped windows with stained glass reminded him of the little church in Spain where they'd taken the men who'd been mortally wounded or had died in the battle. It was the last place he'd seen Marcus's lifeless body before he'd been forced to march on. The emotion was still so fresh---as if the events had happened yesterday. Suddenly his cravat was too tight, like a noose around his neck. His breath was coming fast. He needed to leave. Panic began to rise within him. He didn't want to create a scene, but better to walk out than allow the entire village to witness his weakness and pity him. His fists clenched, and he could feel perspiration gathering on his brow. He had to get some air.

Miraculously, when he looked up, the vicar had just ended his sermon, smiling down at his parishioners. Edward leaned over to his mother. "I'll wait for you by the carriage."

She looked as if about to protest, but he stood and strode toward the door before she could speak. His only thought was getting away from these four walls which were quickly closing in on him.

Once outside, he took great gulps of air and quickly walked to the side of the church. He had to get his emotions under control. Clenching and unclenching his fists, he stared out over the cemetery where his father lay and many of the villagers. Charlotte's father was there as well. Yet, all Edward could think of was the families of his brothers-in-arms who hadn't had a body to bury. No, Edward had left his friends in Spain and marched on.

He closed his eyes, pushing away the dark thoughts. The tightness in his chest was starting to ease from being outside. Feeling anxious to collect his mother and return home, he was surprised to feel a warm hand on his arm.

"Edward?"

He would know that voice anywhere. Opening his eyes, he looked down at the woman next to him. She was worried, her concern evident from the crease between her brows. She moved closer, the hem of her dress hovering quite near his boots. "Are you well?"

No. He definitely was not. Her touch warmed him, even through her gloves, but the pity in her eyes couldn't be tolerated. He stepped back, severing the contact between them. "Perfectly fine, thank you."

The wounded look on her face was nearly more than he could bear. She frowned and tilted her head, as if trying to read his thoughts. "We need to talk."

He couldn't face her. He wasn't strong enough to resist her familiarity. The war had broken him and he wasn't fit for anyone's company, least of all hers. And since she knew him so well, she might see the very things he wanted to hide from her and from the rest of the world. "Pardon me, my lady, but I can't linger. I must see my mother home." He stepped in the direction of the church, but she moved in front of him, blocking his way.

"Your mother already agreed that you should escort me home today." Her chin jutted out in determination. Clearly, she wasn't going to let him go until she had her say.

Edward groaned inwardly, but there wasn't a choice. He couldn't very well refuse Charlotte, especially now that he'd noticed half the parish watching them. If he cut Charlotte now, it would reflect on her reputation. He reluctantly offered his arm. "Shall we?"

She slipped her hand in the crook of his elbow, but didn't press against him as she once did. Her touch was cool and indifferent, as if they were strangers.

In a way, we are, Edward thought. *She just doesn't know it yet.*

They strolled silently to the edge of the village green, nodding to those who couldn't quite hide their stares and smiles. He was beginning to feel as if he were one of the animals in the Royal Menagerie. Everyone seemed to be holding him in some sort of hushed awe.

Finally gaining the road, Edward waited for Charlotte to speak her mind, but she seemed content to merely walk beside him. All too soon, the road that led to her house was in front of them. How many times had he accompanied her home just like this? Walking with her on his arm, felt as if he were walking back in time, before the war.

Before everything had changed. Before *he* had changed.

With Charlotte beside him, he was tempted to pretend that things were as they had once been. That he was free to love her and that their future was bright.

Maybe just for today, he'd allow himself one stolen moment, something he should never have with her—but couldn't resist.

CHAPTER 4

Once they were away from the prying eyes of half the village, Charlotte relaxed. Edward seemed to as well. They walked in silence for a while, enjoying the last of the crisp autumn air that would all too soon turn wintry and cold.

She stole a glance at Edward. He'd always been a handsome man, but walking beside her now, she could see small differences. His shoulders seemed more broad, his chest more defined. He had a bit of stubble on his jaw that added an air of roughness, and suggested his valet had been in a hurry to shave him this morning. Edward also had a scar under his chin that hadn't been there previously. It was strange that she'd known his face nearly as well as her own, but now there were differences she couldn't account for. This thin white scar hadn't been from a scrape they'd gotten into, like the one on the back of his left hand. This one on his chin had likely been from something he'd experienced during the war.

She let out a puff of air, loath to speak and ruin the easiness between them. It wasn't hard to imagine that they were still in love and preparing to be married, while strolling thus on his arm. They turned off the lane and took a path that led to a shortcut between their families' properties. The sky had cleared, and she was right where she'd wanted to be—with Edward. They were even close to the tree where they'd made their solemn promises to each other and said their final goodbyes two years ago. Did he remember? She leaned into his side as she'd always done previously, enjoying their momentary closeness. He felt like home.

Edward apparently did not feel the same, as he pulled away, putting a proper distance between them. "Did David speak to you?"

The few birds that had been singing moments before fell silent at the words. His voice was curt, a tone she'd rarely heard from him in all the years she'd known him. The question cut through her daydream as she crashed back to reality, pain stabbing through her heart.

"Yes, he did." What else could she say?

"It will make things easier for you if you cry off and say we just didn't suit. No one could possibly attach scandal to your name." He stared straight ahead, launching each word like a little dagger to her heart.

She stumbled and barely caught herself from falling in a heap at his feet. He obviously hadn't heard of the scandal her family had already been through in the last few months. If he wasn't pushing her away because of that, then what else could it be?

"Why, Edward? Why are you doing this?" Charlotte pushed down the tears that were threatening to fall. "I don't care what anyone else thinks of us. We *do* suit. We always have. Why don't you want to marry me any longer?"

His steps slowed, and he looked down at her. Sorrow and hurt flashed through his eyes before those emotions were gone, leaving only an empty stare she barely recognized. "I've changed, Charlie. Too many things . . . I can't explain. It's just better this way."

She tightened her grip on his arm, wishing she could hold him to her, show him they could still have a future. "No, it isn't better this way. We've always faced trials together. When your father was so dreadful, we faced his threatenings and punishments together. When my father died, we stood united and you helped with my grief. Let me help you with whatever you're facing now."

"You can't. No one can." He moved across the path and released her. Charlotte's arm fell to her side. "I'm not the man I was." He grimaced and looked away. "Or the man you think me to be."

She stepped closer again, but stopped when he shrank away. What could he mean? "You are exactly the man I think you to be. Nothing could have changed you that drastically. There isn't anything that could alter the love we feel for each other. You promised me that before you left."

His jaw tightened as he stared down the worn path, not meeting her gaze. "We were hardly more than children then. We can't be expected to be held to promises made when we had no idea what we were talking about."

At his condescending tone, frustration rose within her. "Tell me what's changed. Let me stand with you and face whatever it is you think must keep us apart."

"You can't." His tone was so final, it scared her.

No, she wouldn't accept that answer from him. It wasn't over between them. She pointed at the tree to their right. "Do you mean to say when you pledged your sacred honor to come back for me, to make me your wife, and sealed your vow with a kiss right over there, with the heavens as our witness, that was just childish dreams and foolish promises?"

He swallowed, but met her gaze. "Yes."

She shook her head. "I've never known you to tell me a falsehood right to my face."

He threw up his hands. "What do you want from me?"

"The truth!" She moved back to his side and said softly, "Please. That's all I ask."

"Nothing I could tell you would be fit for mixed company. I'd just like to be left alone. The sooner you accept that I cannot marry you, the better it will be for all." He looked down at her, his eyes hard. "Sign the papers from the solicitor to dissolve our betrothal, and you won't ever have to hear from me again. We'll both have what we want."

"That's not what I want and I'll never sign those papers." Anger flared through her, and her fingers curled into fists. "If you're going to break our betrothal, then you will have to jilt me and bankrupt my family as you've threatened to do." She whirled around and began to walk down the path. Without even a glance over her shoulder for his help getting over the stile, she bunched her skirts in one hand and mounted the step. His footsteps approached from behind, but she didn't wait and climbed over, jumping down onto the other side. She continued walking, her half boots crunching on the leaves, her emotions grinding them into the ground. How could he do this?

Edward easily caught up and put his hand on her arm until she turned to look at him. His mouth had dropped open, and he was shaking his head. "You can't possibly mean that. I couldn't allow. . ."

She arched a brow, not slowing down her steps at all. "You can't jilt me because it would call your honor into question? Is that it? Or is it seeing my family beggared that bothers you? If our betrothal was just a childish whim to you and you're so anxious to be rid of me, I don't see why it would matter to you at all."

He snapped his mouth closed and looked away. "Your family has nothing to fear from me. But jilting you would take away any chance for you to find happiness with someone else. The scandal would ruin you."

Charlotte lifted her chin, wishing she dared to make him look at her. The fact that he still cared about her reputation told her that the old Edward was still inside. Somewhere. And she was determined to find him.

"I don't want anyone else, Edward. If you are truly breaking our betrothal, then I'll remain a spinster." She couldn't hold back her emotions any longer, and the tears began to roll down her cheeks. She swiped them away. "I've known since I was in pinafores that you were the one for me. There will never be anyone else."

She stopped at the fork in the path---the left led to Hartwell Manor, the right to Winslow Hall. Their tree was just behind them, where they'd shared so many stolen moments. The memories washed over her. "Do you remember how happy we were when our parents agreed to our marriage and the formal papers were signed? We couldn't wait to be man and wife."

She wanted so badly to be in his arms, for him to say this was all a terrible dream, and to wake up to the smiling face of the man she'd once promised to marry.

Edward stared at her, his face stricken. "Don't cry." He reached out a hand as if to wipe away her tears, before he realized what he was doing and snatched it back. "Charlie. I can't marry you. Or anyone." His voice was low and strangled. "I'm sorry. I just can't." He bowed and walked away, his boots striding quickly over the ground as he took the fork in the road that led to his home.

Charlotte watched him go, a flicker of hope in her heart. He wanted her happiness. She'd seen a glimmer of the Edward she knew and loved. He'd even called her Charlie. There was still something between them. She could feel it.

It wasn't over yet, no matter what he said.

CHAPTER 5

*E*verything inside Edward wanted to march straight back to Charlotte and hold her close, maybe even kiss her and tell her how much he would always love her.

But he couldn't.

He'd known he wasn't strong enough. He should have come up with some excuse not to escort her home today. Yet, he'd wanted to be near her. A part of him even wanted to confess what was troubling him, but he would never burden her with the darkness he now carried inside. He clenched his fists and forced himself to keep moving toward the manor house. He dreaded going indoors. If his mother had given her blessing to walking Charlotte home, she would be hoping for a happy report. One more thing he couldn't give her.

Instead of facing that unhappy meeting with his mother, he turned and headed for the stables. Opening the door, the familiar smells of leather and horse greeted him, and he relaxed a bit. When he'd lived at home, riding had been his one escape from his father. He needed that escape again today.

He walked down the row of stalls, looking at the fine horses who still resided at the estate. His father had always been proud of his choices in horseflesh. When Edward came to the end of the row, Owen, the stablemaster sat on a stool, polishing a bridle. He looked surprised, but stood at Edward's entrance and bobbed his head. "My lord."

Owen had hardly changed. He'd been employed by the family for as long as Edward could remember and had been the one to teach Edward to ride. The man had a few more wrinkles bracketing his clear blue eyes now and a little gray streaked his dark hair. But his calm demeanor, which had always soothed small boys learning to ride as well as the horses, was still there.

"Owen. It's good to see you." The man had been more of a father to him than his own father had been. Edward had missed Owen and the horses while he'd been away in Spain, but he pushed those feelings down deep. He didn't want to be reminded of the past. Of how things had been before. He only wanted to forget. "Is there a horse in need of a good, bruising ride?"

"Mephistopheles is always ready for a neck-or-nothing ride, my lord." Owen moved toward the stalls just behind them. A horse that looked to be close to seventeen hands snorted at their approach. "Your father acquired him right before he fell ill. Mephistopheles is a racing horse and he's got a bit of the devil in him."

"Hence the name, I'll wager." A horse named after a demon was perfect for how Edward felt today. He joined Owen at the stall door. The horse was a satiny black, his eyes staring at them in defiance. He pawed the ground as if daring them to get out of his way so he could run.

Exactly the horse Edward needed.

He reached out a hand so Mephistopheles could sniff it, and

after a long blink and another snort, Mephistopheles walked forward. He smelled Edward's hand, then tossed his head in approval. "Have him saddled immediately."

Owen nodded and seemed about to say something more, but Edward turned on his heel to wait outside. He didn't want to converse with anyone or risk talking about the past. Speaking with Charlotte had already stirred up feelings best left buried. He just wanted to be alone and forget. Forget the war, forget Charlotte, forget everything.

It didn't take long for Owen to bring the horse to him saddled and ready to ride. The old stablemaster didn't speak, merely gave him a smart bow before delivering the reins into Edward's hands and departing. Edward was glad, but a small bit of his conscience whispered that he owed his stablemaster more---some conversation, a kind word, a fond remembrance. He couldn't. Not anymore. He had to stay detached and alone. He didn't dare get close to anyone and possibly poison any goodness they had in them.

Mounting the horse, Edward flicked the reins and headed for the edge of the property. As soon as he had some running room, he kicked the horse into a gallop, bending low in the seat. Mephistopheles seemed to sense Edward's need for speed, and his hooves flew over the ground in a flat-out run. The grass and trees were a blur, the wind in his face exhilarating. Being on the back of a horse gave him a sense of freedom he couldn't find anywhere else.

Finally slowing to a canter when he came near the woods, Edward stopped and dismounted. It was an easy decision to lead Mephistopheles to the stream that wound its way through the middle of the trees. Edward let the horse drink his fill while he looked around at the familiar woods that filled him with memories. He'd spent nearly every day in these trees with Charlotte,

David, and Marcus during the summer months until he'd been sent away to school. They'd built forts, pretended to hunt lions, and had mock battles.

Edward sighed and tugged at his cravat. Marcus had always planned on joining the army. As the son of a steward, he'd had the choice of following in his father's footsteps, or making his own way. Marcus had wanted the adventure and glory of being a soldier, and had often talked of how it would be to wear the uniform and serve his country. Edward never had the luxury of choosing his own path. That had been done for him the moment he'd been born the heir to a viscount.

But when Marcus had declared he was volunteering for the army and leaving the next day, Edward had decided then and there to join him. The thought of being away from his father's influence and making his own decisions had seemed exciting, but that one fateful choice had changed the course of his life forever. And once he'd joined Marcus on the battlefield, nothing had been as he'd thought. He hadn't been prepared for the sacrifices that had to be made and the scenes of carnage he'd witnessed. As boys they'd dreamed of glory and coming home hailed as the heroes who'd saved England. But those dreams had burned away like dew in the sunshine. There was no glory in soldiering.

Edward tied the horse to a tree and sat down on a large flat rock that Charlotte had always called her thinking rock. Did she still come here? Seeing her today had brought on a rush of feelings he'd rather avoid. She was right when she'd said they both knew they were meant to be together. He'd known that since he was a lad. Charlotte saw the man he'd wanted to become and had pushed him to be that man. She had a laugh that was contagious and lips that tempted him beyond all reason. But he couldn't have her now, knowing the darkness that had become part of his soul during the war. How could he sully her with it?

The peace he craved didn't appear even after watching the stream burble below him for a time, but the sun was beginning to sink toward the horizon. Time to go home. With a sigh he got off the rock and started to walk back to the house. Hartwell contained so many memories. They overwhelmed him. Perhaps he should go back to London. At least there he wouldn't feel the disappointment of his mother and Charlotte so keenly---and witness it on their faces.

Mounting the horse once more, Edward rode slowly back to the stables. Exhaustion was stealing over him, and he wanted to retreat to his room. When he walked through the front door, however, his mother called from the blue drawing room, where she usually received her guests for tea. "Edward, is that you? I must speak with you."

Rubbing his hand over his face, he took a breath. He should have known she'd be waiting. "Yes, Mother." He walked into the room as if he were about to face a court-martial and knew he would be found guilty.

She smiled when he entered, and he was once again struck by how beautiful she was, even dressed in unrelenting black. In her day, she must have been the most sought-after debutante of the season, and she'd weathered the years since with nary a wrinkle. Even her blonde hair didn't seem to have any gray in it yet.

"There you are." She patted the seat next to her on the settee. "Did you have a pleasant walk with Charlotte? I expected you hours ago, but hoped that you were taking the time to get reacquainted. Come and tell me all about it."

Edward's stomach sank. He didn't want to have this conversation now, but it seemed he must. So he moved to her side and sat in the proffered seat.

She turned to the table beside her, reaching for a plate so she could begin filling it for him. "I thought you might be hungry after being out for so long, so I ordered a tea tray." She handed him the plate full of his favorite sandwiches and biscuits. "Don't keep me in suspense. Charlotte has been looking forward to your home-coming for months. Was it a happy reunion for both of you?" She smiled expectantly, her hands clasped together as if she were waiting for some wonderful news.

"Mother, you put me in a very awkward position." His voice came out sterner than he would have liked. The smile on her face faded away. *Blast*.

"Whatever do you mean?" Her hand fluttered to her throat, her eyes uncertain.

"I won't be marrying Charlotte." His mother frowned and opened her mouth to protest, but he held up a hand. "Or anyone. I wish you had spoken to me first before volunteering me to escort Charlotte home. I was waiting for the right time to speak to her about breaking our betrothal, but my hand was forced today." He shifted in his seat, remembering the wounded look in Charlotte's eyes. His heart twisted again.

"Break your betrothal? But why?" His mother snapped her mouth shut, obviously trying to cover her shock. She reached for her tea, but changed her mind and sat back in her chair and folded her hands in her lap. "You have only ever had eyes for each other. Charlotte has waited faithfully, even with all the turmoil in her life. She's looked forward to your return with such enthusiasm." Her shoulders drooped. "Whyever would you cast her off?"

His mind could only latch onto one word his mother had uttered. "Turmoil? What turmoil has Charlotte had in her life?" She was an earl's sister, received in all the best circles. What turmoil could there possibly have been? But his mind recalled faint whispers about David and his family months ago, though he couldn't recall exactly what they'd been.

His mother turned her face away at his question and Edward's heart sank. "What's happened?"

"It's so difficult to speak of." She looked away and took a deep breath. "Several months ago, Lord Pembroke accompanied Charlotte to London for some diversion while you were away, but he became embroiled in a murder investigation. He was a suspect!" Her eyes snapped to his, wide with shock at what she'd shared. "I've known David Pembroke since he was in leading strings, and I knew he couldn't possibly have murdered anyone. But the *ton* turned their backs on him." Her voice lowered, sadness coloring her tone. "And as his sister, they turned on Charlotte as well. She was given the cut direct by people she'd thought to be her friends. A week later David brought Charlotte home and she's mostly been in seclusion ever since."

"Was David proven innocent?" Edward could hardly believe what he was hearing. David had always been a jovial fellow who liked to wager a bit too much, but he loved his mother and sister. It seemed incomprehensible he'd be accused of murder.

"Yes, the true murderer was caught, but the damage to the Pembroke family had already been done." His mother shook her head. "Charlotte has continued to be the cheerful girl I've always known, but the last months have been hard for her. Even some villagers have refused her charity."

Edward couldn't stay seated any longer. "That is ridiculous. A false accusation can't trump years of knowing a person! Who is it that is treating her badly? I'll speak with them." How dare they? He paced in front of his mother. Charlotte was the kindest and most genuine person he'd known. The villagers knew that. Most of the *ton* knew that as well. She didn't deserve to be treated with anything but respect.

"Now you can see why she's been looking forward to your return. You've been her closest friend and someone she could count on for most of her life. And now you're telling me that you've turned your back on her as well?" His mother's eyes shone bright with unshed tears. Edward tensed. He couldn't bear to make his mother cry.

"I would never turn my back on her, Mother. I just can't marry her." If only he could make her understand. Her and Charlotte both.

His mother pulled a handkerchief out of her sleeve and dabbed at her eyes. "She's lost so much. I don't know how she'll bear losing you, too."

Edward resumed his pacing. There had to be something he could do. But what? "Maybe it would be best for everyone if I returned to London. Putting some distance between us might make ending our betrothal easier."

His mother frowned. "Nothing will make that easier and you leaving could damage her reputation further. She loves you, Edward."

Her words echoed what Charlotte had said to him earlier, and his heart squeezed. "It can't be helped, I'm afraid."

"Please don't go back to London until after the Christmas holidays." His mother stood and reached out to touch his arm. "No matter what has happened with Charlotte, I've only just gotten you home after years of waiting and worrying. I'd hate for your visit to be cut short. I want to know you again."

Her imploring eyes made it impossible to say no. "Very well. I'll stay until after the Christmas holidays. Perhaps by then I can work out the details with David to end the betrothal so Charlotte can be free to move on."

His mother shook her head. "She'll never be free of her love for you," she said softly.

Edward stiffened. He wouldn't ever be free of his love for her either, but that wasn't something he could voice. He merely nodded. "I hope, for her sake, that's not true."

Though a small part of him rejoiced that maybe, just maybe, he would always have a tiny piece of Charlotte's heart that could never be claimed by anyone else.

CHAPTER 6

There was a cold bite in the air, but Charlotte welcomed it as she started on her walk home from the village. Mrs. Atherton had been grateful for the basket of bread and jellies, along with the booties and matching baby blanket she'd made.

This visit had gone better than the one she'd endured a few weeks ago with Mrs. Lindstrom. They'd both taken tea with the vicar's wife and Charlotte had looked forward to socializing with friends. But not long into the visit, Mrs. Lindstrom had announced that her sister worked for a fine house in London and had written to share that Charlotte's good name had been tainted by scandal. Of course, Mrs. Lindstrom never came out and said anything truly offensive that afternoon, but her disdainful sniffs and comments about how important a good reputation is to a lady, had grated on Charlotte's nerves.

The vicar's wife had done her best to quell any more rumors, but the damage had already been done. Most of the villagers still treated Charlotte the same as they always had, but a few of the ladies seemed to want to believe the worst of her. It stung, but there wasn't anything Charlotte could do about it.

Charlotte's visit to Mrs. Atherton today had been a balm to her heart. She'd stared down at the tiny baby in her arms. His downy hair and sleepy sighs had soothed her bruised heart. The sight of that precious, innocent face had made her forget, for just a moment, any of the problems she'd had in the village or with Edward. All she'd seen was a sleeping baby snuggled close to her chest, safe in her arms.

For years she'd dreamed of the children she'd have with Edward, that they would finally be a family, but that seemed far off now, if not impossible. With that thought stealing into her moment with the baby, she'd let out a slow breath before giving the newborn back to his mother and bidding Mrs. Atherton goodbye.

Crunching through the leaves on her walk home, Charlotte got a bit of satisfaction grinding them into the packed dirt, letting out some frustration in a ladylike way. She was so confused. The past six months had been so difficult. The excitement of going to London had been dashed after being ostracized after her brother's murder accusation. The anticipation of Edward's homecoming had been extinguished by his apparent change of heart, though deep inside she believed he still cared for her. Coming to their country home had seemed a blessing---a retreat from the trials she was experiencing, but now everything was all a muddle. Did Edward want to break the betrothal because of something she'd done? What was the true reason?

With no answers, and the wind starting to swirl around her skirts, she decided to take the shortcut. Though she wanted to avoid any reminders of the words she'd had with Edward after church on Sunday, the overgrown path that divided her family's land from Edward's would cut down her walking time considerably.

She retraced the steps she'd taken with him after church and climbed over the wooden stile before walking briskly toward the trees. She deliberately avoided looking at their special tree as she approached. Her heart was too raw today for many reminders of how happy she'd once been, with many of her most joyful moments happening right under the branches of the old oak.

Despite her best intentions, however, she looked anyway. The few leaves left were clinging hopelessly to the branches, but the wind was winning the war, bringing them swiftly to the ground. As if the tree was silently warning her to hurry, she glanced up at the clouds to see that a storm looked to be on its way. She would definitely prefer to be home before it started. She quickened her steps.

Just as she reached the treeline, she heard a whine and stopped. Had it been the wind? She cocked her head to the side and listened. The high-pitched whine came again, just to her left. Cautiously moving toward the sound, she peered down into a small ditch. There, huddled in a ball, was a dog. Two large eyes peered up at her as if the dog was surprised she'd come.

"Oh you poor thing!" She stepped down into the ditch and squatted next to the animal. Deciding to take every precaution, Charlotte held out her hand so the dog could sniff it, but the obviously miserable creature could barely lift her head. She whined again, and Charlotte's eyes were drawn to the dog's matted hair, scrawny body, and a wound on her bloody back paw. Looking for any other wounds and deciding that was the only one, Charlotte reached back for her basket. She took out the crust of bread that had fallen to the bottom. "It's not much, girl."

She held out her offering, and the dog nibbled at it but was too exhausted to do more. Charlotte petted the poor animal's head while the dog closed her eyes. "I don't know how you got here, but I'm going to help you out of this predicament."

But how could she get the dog to the house? The animal didn't look like she weighed much, but Charlotte was still a mile or more away from the estate. As if on cue, hoofbeats sounded behind her, and she quickly stood to ask the unknown rider for assistance. "I'll get us some help, girl," she promised.

Raising her hand to signal the rider, her arm froze in mid-air. She knew that form. Edward.

He'd spotted her and turned his horse in her direction, his eyes piercing. "Charlotte." He took in her muddy dress and hands. "Are you all right?"

She brushed off her hands, wishing she could brush off the feelings he evoked in her middle just as easily. "Yes, I'm quite all right. But I do need your assistance." At his raised eyebrows, she moved back so he could see the dog. "I need to get this poor creature home."

Edward shook his head, a smile spreading across his face. "I should have known. Still saving all the wounded animals you find. The woodland creatures must know of your reputation. Even this poor thing has made its way to the border of your estate."

He dismounted and approached her. They both looked down at the dog. "Dirty, hungry, and the back leg could use some bandaging." He stared at the path in front of them, as if working something out in his mind. "Hartwell is closer than Winslow Hall. We'll take her there."

Charlotte nodded, absurdly pleased to have him use "we" and include her in his plans. As he always had before. "Lead the way."

Edward took off his coat and bent to wrap the dog in it. She whimpered, but once she was in Edward's arms, she seemed to relax. "Don't worry about a thing, old girl," Edward murmured.

He walked toward his horse and Charlotte followed.

"Mephistopheles is strong enough to carry all three of us home, but mounting will be tricky." He handed her the bundle in his arms. "I'll mount first, then pull you up."

Charlotte did not see how this was going to work, but she stood there obediently holding the muddy dog while he mounted the horse. "Can you hold her in one arm while I hoist you up?"

Charlotte adjusted the dog who was looking up at her with such an air of trust, she didn't dare let her down. "Yes, I think I can do that."

Reaching out, she took Edward's hand. His palms were callused now and the strength in his arms easily pulled her onto his lap. Sitting close to him felt so familiar and right, it made her chest ache. This was where she'd wanted to be every day since he'd left. She pulled in a breath and could barely resist laying her head on his shoulder. He smelled of sandalwood and leather and male warmth. She'd dreamed so often of his particular scent. It was as wonderful as she remembered.

Oblivious to her turmoil, Edward adjusted her across his lap. "Are you settled?"

Charlotte didn't trust her voice. She was quite unsettled, actually, but nodded in the affirmative anyway. They started toward Hartwell, and Charlotte didn't mind being pressed into Edward's chest. He put one arm around her waist to steady her and kept the reins in his other. Her heart pounded at his closeness, his broad shoulders shielding her from the elements. Charlotte closed her eyes, reveling in the feeling of being cherished and protected, even for but a moment.

The dog stirred and Charlotte looked down at her precious cargo. The injured animal must have felt as comfortable as Charlotte, lulled to sleep by the horse's motion and safe in Edward's keeping. At least Charlotte hoped she was asleep. Alarm ran through her at the question, so she put her fingers near the dog's nose and gave a sigh of relief. She was still alive.

Edward's voice was low in her ear. "She'll be fine. Don't worry."

Charlotte shivered. The dog might be fine, but Charlotte wasn't sure she would be. She wanted Edward with her, close like this, just how they'd always planned. But all too soon Hartwell came into view and a groom walked out to greet them. Edward positioned her just right so he could dismount first, then reached back for her. Putting his hands on her waist, he lifted her off the horse as if she weighed no more than a feather---even with a dog in her arms. Edward looked down at her for a long moment, and she could see naked longing in his eyes and her heart leapt. She moved closer, wanting to show him she felt the same.

Opening her mouth to say his name, he dropped his gaze to the ground and bowed slightly, stepping back before she could get a word out. "Let's take her to the kitchen," he said, his voice gruff. The groom led the horse away, and Edward started off toward the house.

Disappointed, Charlotte numbly followed him to the servants' entrance. Opening the door, they stopped in the small entryway to wipe their feet. Mrs. Blackhurst, the cook at Hartwell since Edward was a baby, had never taken kindly to muddy feet in her kitchen. Going down the small hallway, they entered the warm room. Mrs. Blackhurst was sitting at the table with a cup of tea in her hand.

"What have we here?" she asked, setting her teacup aside and standing as quickly as her large girth would allow.

"Lady Charlotte has a patient in need of some doctoring." Edward took the dog from her arms and moved closer to the fire. "Can you have a tub of water readied and some food suitable for a dog? Oh, and a bandage."

Mrs. Blackhurst shook her head. "Just like old times, the two of you bringing in an injured animal. Remember the time you found the crow with the broken wing? You brought it inside and it put up a terrible fuss, squawking and jumping all over my kitchen."

"But that was a success story," Charlotte exclaimed. "Once we made a proper cage and splinted the wing in place, that crow healed nicely. It flew away a few weeks later."

"Not before I made a vow not to treat wounded animals in my kitchen again." Mrs. Blackhurst *tsked*, and her hands went to her ample hips. "Since this is a dog, however, I'll make an exception." She bustled out of the room to get the things Edward had asked for.

Edward grinned at Charlotte. "That bird gave Mrs. Blackhurst such a fright, she talked about it for months as if we'd brought the devil himself into the house. She was convinced he was a cursed bird."

"I remember." Charlotte gingerly sat in the chair near the fire. Hopefully Mrs. Blackhurst wouldn't mind a bit of mud from her dress getting on her clean floors. She didn't want to be in the cook's black books any more than she was. She glanced over at Edward. "I was glad the poor crow couldn't fly very well or we really would have been in trouble."

Edward laughed. "As if you could ever get in trouble with that innocent face of yours." He patted the dog's head. "No one could stay angry with you. Not your parents or your brother. Or me."

His last two words hung in the air and the happy mood turned somber. Was he angry with her, but couldn't reconcile the feeling because of their past? Before Charlotte could question him, Mrs. Blackhurst walked back into the room, carrying a medium-size tin tub. "I had some water heated up for your bath, Master Edward. But I suppose you won't mind sacrificing some for your patient."

Edward hung his head and let out a long-suffering sigh. "What kind of wretch would I be if I said I did?" With his lips curved in a half smile, he lifted the dog into his arms once more and brought her to the table. Charlotte followed close behind. Would the animal protest the bath? Mrs. Blackhurst wouldn't let them step foot in her kitchen again if they had another animal mishap. Charlotte was apprehensive as Edward laid the dog gently in the water, but the dog merely looked at them, her eyes soft. Was she too exhausted to care what happened to her? So hungry she had no energy? Charlotte's heart welled with compassion. What if she hadn't taken the shortcut home? This poor dog would have died.

Without a word, Edward and Charlotte worked together to bathe the dog, soaping the matted fur until the water was nearly black. When they lifted her out of it, her fur was actually a light tan instead of dark brown. After drying her off with a length of cloth, Charlotte wrapped her in it and moved toward the fire again.

Mrs. Blackhurst clucked as she took the tub away. "Poor mite. I put some water for it in a bowl and a bit of meat on a plate just there."

Charlotte held the dog close to her chest, hoping the fire would take away any remaining chill. Edward retrieved the food. Kneeling in front of her, he offered the meat to the dog who opened her eyes and licked it. After a few more tries, she managed to take a bite and lap up a little water before drifting back to sleep.

"Should we bandage her leg, do you think?" Charlotte asked. He nodded and she moved to transfer the dog into Edward's arms, but he motioned for her to stay still.

He stepped forward and picked up the bandage Mrs. Blackhurst had placed on the small table next to the chair. With practiced precision, he bandaged the leg and tied the ends off. He'd done it so quickly, Charlotte was surprised. She'd usually been the one to bandage any rescued animals. He'd never liked to look at the wounds.

"Where did you learn to do that?" she asked, staring down at the perfectly even edges.

His eyes went to the dog. "There were plenty of opportunities to help take care of wounded men after a battle, but there was this dog." He swallowed. His voice was tight, but he went on. "That dog hung around camp for scraps and followed us as closely as he could. There was a skirmish one night . . . the dog was wounded. I tried everything I could think of . . . but I couldn't save him."

His voice faded away and Charlotte wished she hadn't asked. "I'm so sorry, Edward."

He stood. "It's no matter. It was just an animal."

Edward stepped back, putting physical distance between them. The hollow look in his face had reappeared, emphasizing that the emotional distance they'd bridged today had also returned. His lips were a flat line, and all traces of laughter and familiarity were gone. "Just leave the dog in Mrs. Blackhurst's care. I'll go make sure a carriage is readied to take you home."

"I can walk," she said quietly. "I don't want to inconvenience you." But now that the room was so still, Charlotte could hear the howling wind and rain hitting the house.

"It's not an inconvenience at all." He inched toward the door. "Always a pleasure to see you, my lady."

And he quit the room.

Charlotte sat there with the sleeping dog in her lap, letting sadness and shock roll over her. Seeing glimpses of the Edward she knew gave her hope that her dreams could still come true. But when moments like this happened, when his memories of the war surfaced and the old Edward vanished, he became someone she didn't recognize. She was just like the wind and rain outside, howling their protest and pounding against the barrier keeping them from getting inside.

Was it time she acknowledged the inevitable? That no matter

what she said or did, the Edward she knew was gone? Her heart said no, but if he was so determined not to try to work through whatever was plaguing him, she might not have a choice.

And that was one thing she didn't know if she could ever accept.

CHAPTER 7

*E*dward sat in the library staring out into the darkness. If he looked hard enough, he could almost imagine he saw the chimneys of Charlotte's home, but it was merely imagination. He took another drink of brandy from the glass in his hand. Seeing her today had brought back so many happy childhood memories that for just a moment, he'd forgotten the guilt and sadness that were his constant companions now. How he wished he could shake them, but it was clear they were part of his penance.

The door creaked open, but Edward didn't turn around. He wasn't in the mood to speak to anyone. Hopefully it was just a maid coming in to build up the fire. Swirling the last of the drink in his hand, he took another sip and, when a furry body brushed against his leg, nearly spit it out. Looking down, he saw the dog they'd rescued earlier that day.

"How'd you get in here?" he asked, bending down to scratch the dog behind the ears. She looked up, her brown eyes watching him closely, as if asking what *he* was doing in here.

He patted her head and she wagged her tail. Her ribs were still visible, but her fur was clean and the color reminded him of his favorite tan breeches. Edward stood and turned away from the window, walking toward the chair closest to the fire. The dog followed and waited until he sat on the wingback, before lying down at his feet. Edward reached out to pet her again, but the image of the dog he'd befriended in Spain came unbidden to his mind. He decided against it and drew his hand back. He didn't want to get attached to her. He'd rescued and claimed that dog, too, and it had ended badly. He had hardly been able to speak of the incident to Charlotte today without swallowing a lump in his throat.

Draining the rest of his brandy, he stared at the small embers glowing in the hearth, feeling cowardly. He didn't want to risk opening his heart again, not even to an animal, and especially not to Charlotte. In his state, he couldn't take any more losses of those he cared for. But the dog had been through a difficult experience and looked so comfortable by the fire. As much as he should, he didn't want to summon a servant to have her removed, so he settled in. He was more like the dog than he cared to admit. The animal's scars were on the outside and needed care, while Edward's wounds were on his soul. The difference was that the dog had allowed others to come to her aid. Edward couldn't do that. What could anyone do for the scars he carried on his heart? There was no tincture, bandage, or potion to heal that.

His mind turned to Charlotte and all the animals she'd rescued over the years. They always did seem drawn to her, as if they knew she would help them and be gentle about it. Riding with her in his arms had felt as wondrous as he'd imagined, and he'd cherished every second he had with her. From the way she'd relaxed and nearly snuggled into his chest, Charlotte had enjoyed it, too. But, no matter how much he craved her company, he couldn't allow those kinds of indulgences. It would only hurt her when their betrothal came to an end.

"There you are." His mother walked into the room, her eyes taking in the picture of him relaxed by the fireplace with a dog. She held out a hand as he started to get up. "No, no, don't bother yourself. Mrs. Blackhurst told me that you and Charlotte attempted another rescue today. Is this the animal?"

He glanced at the dog. "Attempted? I'd say we accomplished the rescue. And yes, this is the dog."

"She looks like she's made herself at home and is very comfortable at your feet." His mother sat in the chair opposite him and arranged her skirts. "But also needs a few good meals."

Edward agreed and sank lower in his chair without disturbing the dog. "I didn't have the heart to wake her up. We've both had quite a day."

"Oh, really?" He could almost see his mother's ears perking up at the hint of a story. "Did Charlotte stay long?"

Edward nearly smiled. His mother was more obvious than a Frenchman in a Spanish countryside. But he couldn't acknowledge her well-intended machinations when he knew his answer would be such a disappointment for her. "No. I called the carriage so she wouldn't get soaked walking home in the rainstorm."

His mother frowned. "You could have invited her to stay for tea."

"I couldn't." He met his mother's eyes. "I don't want her to misunderstand my intentions."

With a sigh, his mother sat back in her chair. "Edward . . . No. No, I promised myself I wouldn't say anything more on the subject." But she folded her arms and stared at him, silently communicating her disapproval. "It's just that she's such a good woman and you were happy with her once."

That was exactly the heart of the matter. She was good. And his soul felt as black as soot. He didn't want any of the blackness to touch her. Edward shook his head. "Thank you for abiding by my wishes when it comes to Charlotte. I just need time to sort things out with her, and the circumstances being what they are right now, doing so might take longer than I thought to bring the betrothal to an end. Be patient. That's all I ask."

"I am trying." His mother unfolded her arms and tapped her fingers on the edges of the chair. She took a deep breath. "I did seek you out to ask a favor, actually. I'm wondering if I might have your escort to the Harvest Ball tomorrow night."

The Harvest Ball was really more of a small country dance, but it had always been a highlight for the Walsham village after the harvest. Mixing the local gentry with the villagers made for a merry time, but Edward didn't think he would be able to face them yet. These were people who knew him well, and he valued their good opinion. As his father had reminded him repeatedly, he had a responsibility to those who depended on him for a living.

He tilted his head toward her, not quite meeting her eyes. "Mother, I don't think that's a good idea. For you or for me. You've just begun your mourning period, and I'm not ready to be in such a public setting yet."

His mother clutched her handkerchief in one hand. "Why? You went to church services, and everyone was glad to see you home and whole. And even though we're in mourning for your father, the villagers still wanted to do you a special honor to welcome you after fighting so bravely for your country."

In that case, he definitely didn't want to go. He hadn't been brave. And Marcus's father would be the first to agree. "Perhaps appearing at the ball would be too scandalous when we're in mourning."

"Nonsense. I won't be dancing, of course, and will be dressed in my mourning clothes, but you are the special guest of honor, so the whole village is making an exception." She leaned forward in her chair, her handkerchief nothing more than a crushed scrap of fabric balled in her hand. "They love you, son. Let them give you this honor."

Her eyes glittered in the firelight as if she was holding back tears. Edward couldn't bear it. There was only one answer he could give. "Of course I'll escort you."

His mother sniffed but gave him a smile and leaned over to pat his forearm. "Thank you, son. It means ever so much. I'm so glad you're home."

Edward felt his conscience prick him. He'd been avoiding his mother since he'd come home. Estate business had taken up much of his time, but he should do more than just break his fast with her. "Perhaps I may escort you to the lake tomorrow if the weather holds," he asked. "I know how you like to see the water."

She inclined her head, watching him carefully, her lips curving upward. "That would be wonderful. Thank you."

She stood to leave, and Edward rose with her, waking the dog, who scrambled to her feet and stayed right next to his side as if she were guarding him. "I haven't wanted to mention it before, but when your father realized you weren't coming before he passed away, he wrote you a letter. I promised to deliver it to you." She pulled it from her sleeve and handed it to him. "I'll leave you to your thoughts," his mother said, drawing her shawl closer around her shoulders. "But be careful with the brandy. You'll want a clear head for the ball tomorrow."

Edward bowed politely. "Of course." Kissing her cheek, he bid her goodnight and watched her quit the room before he sat back down in the chair and stared at the sealed parchment in his hand. His father had scrawled his name across the front. When Edward had first run away to join the army, his father had written, but

Edward had had every missive returned, unopened. And he couldn't bear to open this one. Not tonight.

He set it on the table beside him and ran his hand over his eyes. He was so tired but didn't dare sleep. The dog put her paws on his legs, watching him as if to ask for permission before she jumped in his lap. With how thin she was, she barely took up any space at all. Deciding to make them both more comfortable, he stood and lifted her with him before settling on the damask sofa.

He stretched out on his side, with the dog fitting in front of him. Eyeing the decanter of brandy across the room, he was tempted, but didn't get up to pour himself another drink. Instead, he began to stroke the dog's fur. His gaze landed on the brandy again. Did he dare try to sleep without numbing himself first? Since he'd returned to England, the nightmares had grown so disturbing that he often woke screaming, unless he was numbed by alcohol first. But maybe being at Hartwell would help calm that. After all, he'd laughed with Charlotte today. He hadn't laughed since setting foot on English soil. That was progress.

The sofa was soft and comfortable, but the darkness outside was urging him to find his bed and try to sleep. Yet Edward just couldn't do it. His mother's room was near his, and if he woke screaming, it would likely wake her. No, if he was going to see if his nightmares would return while at Hartwell or not, he needed to stay in the library, where he might have a small chance of not waking anyone if he did scream.

Watching the firelight, he petted the dog's back with long, even strokes in a sort of rhythm. Sooner than he expected, his eyelids began to droop, and he didn't fight sleep when it came to him.

Holding the dog close to his side, he drifted off. The dream came right away, as it always did. He was in a field. Only this time, there was no smoke, no cannons, no shouts of men. The field was green, untouched by blood and gore. The sun was shining, and he could hear Charlotte's laughter in the distance.

"Hurry, Edward," she called. "Come and find me."

How could he resist her request? His heart filled with gladness as he started after her, the grass bending as he moved through it. Yes, on some level, Edward knew this was a dream, but he was happy to stay here as long as possible.

"I'm coming," he shouted back. "I'm coming. Wait for me."

And with every fiber of his being, he hoped she would.

CHAPTER 8

$\mathcal{D}$avid, Charlotte, and her mother had arrived at the assembly later than usual. Charlotte's mother hadn't been able to find the particular shawl she'd wanted to wear this evening and the servants had turned the house upside down looking for it. When it had been found in the back of her wardrobe, they'd finally been able to set off. Charlotte had been waiting downstairs near the door, anxious and impatient to get to the assembly, hoping to catch a glimpse of Edward.

When they arrived, she immediately searched the dancers and guests for Edward's familiar form. He wasn't here. Letting out a sigh, she swallowed her disappointment. It was to be expected. His family was in mourning, though the village had hoped the viscount and his mother would consider a small gathering to honor Edward's service not too untoward. Trying to tell herself she could still enjoy being in company, she strolled to the refreshment table. Just as she lifted a glass of tepid lemonade to her lips, a hush went over the crowd.

A tingle went up her spine at the same moment. Edward had arrived.

He was dashing in his regimentals, but looked uncomfortable as the villagers all turned to watch him. He inclined his head, as if to acknowledge the attention, but then started forward to escort his mother into the crowd. Charlotte followed his movements, all of her attention on him. His very presence stirred her, like a magnet pulling her closer. The candlelight made his golden hair look like burnished bronze, and his broad chest and trim waist was emphasized by the cut of his uniform. Her eyes lifted to his face, and their gazes met. He smiled, and Charlotte's heart tripped over itself in response. He escorted his mother in her direction, and she nodded in approval when she saw where they were headed.

Though the crowd tried to pretend they weren't all watching, Charlotte could feel dozens of eyes on her as Edward and his mother approached. Butterflies took wing through her middle, though her feet were rooted to the floor. *Don't be a ninny*, she scolded herself. *He's probably just being polite.*

But he had sought her out nearly the moment he arrived. That had to mean something. In moments, they were in front of her.

"Lady Charlotte," he said as he bowed over her hand. "You look lovely this evening."

Charlotte curtsied. "Thank you, Lord Carlisle. Lady Carlisle."

When she rose, Edward's mother flipped her fan open. "Oh, Edward, I see Lady Bainbridge just there. I'd like to sit and have a coze with her, so don't worry about me. And I do not feel it would be inappropriate for you to dance, seeing as this ball is in your honor." Her eyes widened. "I'm sure Lady Charlotte wouldn't mind stepping onto the dance floor with you, should the opportunity present itself."

Charlotte felt a flush creep up her neck. Of course she would love to dance with Edward, but was his mother forcing him to offer? She didn't want that.

"Yes, Mother." Edward held out his hand in invitation. "Lady Charlotte, may I have this dance?"

Charlotte's heart soared at the thought of being close to him again. "I'd be delighted, my lord."

The next set was just beginning, so they took their places. As she stood across from Edward, their eyes locked, and they drank each other in. He seemed different tonight. Lighter.

A small smile played on Edward's lips as they waited for all the dancers to be in place, but it disappeared when her brother David stood next to Edward, facing the vicar's daughter next to Charlotte. Oh, why had David chosen this dance to stay close to her, when she wanted to be with Edward?

The country dance finally began, and Charlotte tried to ignore her brother. Edward seemed to be doing the same, his only reaction being his jaw visibly clenching. Charlotte stepped forward to take Edward's hand as they moved down the dance line. The spark that had always rushed over her skin whenever they'd touched returned, familiar and somehow stronger.

"How is our patient?" she asked in the few seconds they were close enough for conversation.

"She is well. Enjoying warm fires and plenty of hearty bones from the kitchen." Edward squeezed her fingers before they returned to their places in line. He was nearly his old self, the light in his eyes something she'd sorely missed. Hope kindled in her chest again.

David gave her a quizzical look as they moved around each other, as if silently questioning her, but she refused to acknowledge his glance. She didn't want to hear any comments her brother might have regarding her or Edward.

The dance steps led her back to Edward, and she took his hand again. "I'm surprised Mrs. Blackhurst let the dog stay inside. I was sure she would have been relegated to the stables by now."

"The dog has actually been staying with me in my quarters," Edward said quietly. "She has a calming influence."

Charlotte was surprised to hear his soft admission. She wished they weren't in such a public venue and had the chance to talk in more than fleeting moments between steps. All she could do was nod before she had to move back to her place in line. Knowing the dog they'd rescued was helping Edward in some way warmed her, though. If she couldn't be the one soothing Edward, the dog was the next best thing.

All too soon the dance ended, and Edward was escorting her off the floor. David hurried to walk next to them as they moved toward the chairs near the French doors that led outside. "Are you enjoying being home at Hartwell, Edward?" he asked.

Edward's whole body stiffened. "Of course." Though he claimed enjoyment, his voice was polite and aloof, a tone she'd never heard him use with her or her brother before. She frowned. The light mood she'd been savoring while in Edward's company was slipping away. Quickening her step, she tried to hurry Edward along so David wouldn't have the chance to say anything else, but to no avail.

"Mr. Harper is here." David's words stopped Edward in his tracks, and Charlotte nearly stumbled at their sudden halt. "You do remember Marcus's father?"

Edward's face was stricken, and raw pain shone in his eyes. Charlotte almost fell back at the enormity of it, but then drew closer. Edward obviously needed her.

"Where?" Edward's voice was barely more than a whisper.

"Just there." David nodded toward the exit. "Why haven't you spoken to him since you've been home?"

Edward didn't reply. His head swung to meet the gaze of his

family's old steward and the father of his best friend. Edward's breaths were coming quickly as if he'd been running. He gave her a quick bow. "I apologize, but you must excuse me." Before he could take his leave, however, the vicar stood in front of the musicians and called for everyone's attention.

Though the vicar was a rotund man and short of stature, his voice carried throughout the room. "We are so happy this evening to be favored with Viscount Carlisle's presence. Would that his late father could have been here to celebrate with us, but to have his son return home a war hero is a credit to the Carlisle house and to our village. Welcome home, my lord." He raised his arm and began to shout, "hip, hip hurrah!" and the crowd joined in. They all watched him with smiles on their faces, pride ringing in their cheers, but Charlotte could see the tense lines around Edward's mouth as he stood stone-faced until they'd cheered three times.

"Thank you all," Edward managed as the voices died out. "Thank you for your kindness to my family." With a small bow, he turned on his heel and strode out of the room.

The vicar watched the door, as if he thought that Edward had only stepped out momentarily and expected him back. When that didn't happen, there was an awkward silence. No one moved until the vicar finally motioned for the musicians to begin playing again.

Feeling helpless, Charlotte walked the opposite way and slipped out of the French doors and onto the small terrace. It led out into the village green, but there was an empty bench in a small alcove, so Charlotte started toward it. So many feelings pounded through her veins, she could hardly sort them out. Sitting down, she looked up to the sky. A falling star streaked across the darkness, and she closed her eyes to make a wish.

Please, let Edward see the love he has around him.

She sat there through one set and could hear the musicians beginning a new one. It was past time to go back inside, but she couldn't just yet. The French doors opened again, and Charlotte shrank back into the shadows. She didn't want to talk to anyone right now and wished for a little more time alone. But when she turned and saw Edward leaning over the balustrade, she stood and crossed the small distance between them. He was staring into the darkness, unaware of her approach.

"Edward?" she asked tentatively. Had he returned to the ballroom? Had he spoken to Mr. Harper?

He faced her. His eyes were red-rimmed, as if he'd been trying to hold back tears. She didn't say a word, just wrapped her arms around his waist. He pulled her to him, burying his face in her hair. "Oh, Charlotte. To stand there in front of Marcus's father and be called a hero was nearly intolerable." He drew in a deep breath. "I couldn't save him. I swear I couldn't save him, but I would give anything to go back and give my life for his."

"His death is not your fault. You did all you could." She hugged him tighter, wishing she could take his pain away. "Marcus was your best friend. He knew you loved him and would have given your life for his, just as he would have given his life for yours."

"It should have been me." His words were hardly more than a whisper, but sounded loud in the silence.

"No." Her gut wrenched at even the thought of him hurt or dead. She'd worried for months, especially when his letters stopped.

"I told him to stay close to me, but we got separated during the battle. Afterward, I searched the field and the tents and couldn't find him, so I went to the church where the dead and fatally wounded had been taken. I spent what seemed like hours looking at every face. Marcus was in one of the last pews, with blood everywhere. I called for the medic, but there were too many wounded. All I could do was stay with him and hold his hand until he drew his last breath." He gulped, and his voice trembled. "How can I tell his father that his only son died waiting for someone to attend his injuries? And all that I did was sit there and watch him die?"

"Marcus's father would understand. I know he would." Her heart nearly broke. The pain in his voice was almost too much to bear.

"How could I excuse the fact that I failed him? Before we left, Mr. Harper asked me to look out for Marcus. I promised I would. I tried, heaven knows I tried, but I couldn't keep my word." Edward's eyes were full of anguish. "If I hadn't wanted to get away from my father so badly, Marcus might have been convinced to wait a little longer before joining up. Then he wouldn't have been sent to the front lines in Spain. If I'd been able to stay close to him, to watch over him, he would be alive and home with his father where he belongs." He turned to face the night again, raising his eyes to the sky as if to rage into the blackness with his sorrow and grief. "How can I face anyone in this village who call me a hero, never mind you or Marcus's father?"

She slipped her arms around his back, hugging her to him. "Because we love you. Because it wasn't your fault. Marcus died on the battlefield, along with thousands of other English soldiers. You were lucky enough to be spared, and now you can keep Marcus's memory alive. We both can."

He faced her once again and his hand spanned her cheek. "I don't deserve anyone's love. There is too much pain and darkness in me now."

His thumb caressed her jawline, and she shivered, not from cold, but from the sensations skimming across her skin. "Let love heal your heart, Edward."

He groaned softly. "Charlotte."

His voice was a plea and she answered it by lifting her face to his. He bent to kiss her. His lips were soft and tentative at first, but

Charlotte wanted more, wanted to show him how worthy he truly was of her love. Pressing closer, she wrapped her arms around his neck and deepened the kiss. His hands roamed over her back and into her hair. Charlotte felt as if her nerve endings were on fire and attuned to Edward's every movement. There was nothing else in the world but them and the meeting of their lips, the closeness of their bodies. This is what she'd dreamed of for so long.

"Charlotte," he breathed. "When I'm with you, I believe in redemption."

"Then stay with me always." She reached up on tiptoe and framed his face in her hands. He kissed her again, and she was lost. Lost in sensation. Lost in love.

But the loud gasp that filled the air behind them was like a cold bucket of water. The vicar's wife tittered and said, "Well, Lord Carlisle, I guess we'll be calling the banns as soon as possible."

Charlotte froze. The voice and sentiment grated on her ears. She knew the vicar's wife meant well, but looking into Edward's face, the hollowness was back and he was pulling away again. She almost panicked at his withdrawal when they'd made so much progress tonight, so she reached out her hand, wanting to assure him that she hadn't wanted this to happen. She wanted him to choose her, not be forced to go through with their betrothal if he didn't want her. But the bleakness in his eyes already told her what she needed to know. He would do the honorable thing, no matter what he did or didn't feel.

"Charlotte?" David asked, stepping forward. She slowly turned to face him, wishing she would have heard the door open or taken Edward somewhere else to talk. But what was done was done. "Edward?" David looked between the two of them, obviously worried.

"We were getting reacquainted," Charlotte offered, not daring to glance back at Edward.

"I think we all saw that." The vicar grinned, his hand covering his large belly, watching them like a proud papa. He moved forward to stand beside his wife. "I'm so pleased to see a young couple in love. We should have called the banns this last week from the looks of things." He winked, and Charlotte inwardly winced.

Edward inhaled sharply and put his hands behind his back. "I'm honored to be betrothed to Lady Charlotte and having her as my wife will be a credit to my name. Lord Pembroke, I'll be over in the morning to update the marriage settlements." He bowed to her. "Lady Charlotte."

He took her hand and kissed the back of it, but it was brief, and the warmth between them had turned as cold as the evening air around them.

She needed to speak with him in private, but knew they wouldn't have a moment alone now. "Lord Carlisle, I'd be happy to receive you tomorrow." Maybe if he came, they could talk then. Tell him they could wait until he was ready.

David held out his arm, and she took it. "We'll see you tomorrow," he said, as they walked past Edward and went back into the ballroom.

The vicar and his wife were smiling broadly, and Charlotte gave them a weak smile in return.

"We'll find Mother and return home immediately," David told her. He sounded as resigned as Charlotte felt. They'd been forced to accept so much of society's reproach heaped upon their family in recent months, that no matter how they tried to stem the rumors, they were relentless and insurmountable. Would they ever stop? She was thoroughly weary of trying to make people see the truth.

As if to prove her point, they passed Mrs. Lindstrom on their way to the matron's corner. She shook her head at Charlotte and lifted her fan to whisper to the woman next to her. Charlotte's stomach sank. Would there always be petty rumors and gossip concerning her? She lengthened her stride, nearly pulling David along with her. She wanted to go home. Now.

Her life had irrevocably changed just a few short minutes ago on the terrace. She was about to get what she'd always wanted---to be Edward's wife---but at what cost?

CHAPTER 9

*E*dward rode the familiar drive lined with oak trees that led to Charlotte's house. It was early yet and he'd only just broken his fast. The scones and jelly were sitting like lead in his belly at the moment, though. He was anxious about his interview with David. He hadn't treated David as the friend he was since he'd returned home to England.

Instead, Edward had regarded David as an enemy for mounting a resistance to Edward's aim to break his betrothal to Charlotte. At the time, all he could think of was making sure that no woman was ever shackled to him. David had stood in the way. Edward had threatened and bullied his way to buying up David's vowels for leverage and disdained any attempt David made to reach out. Shame crinkled on the edges of his consciousness, but he'd done what he thought was right.

Deciding he couldn't wait to face his interview with David, he was calling at a very early hour---too early for propriety's sake. He had to get it done now. Reaching the stone steps that led up to Winslow Hall, he dismounted and gave the reins to a groom. He stared up at the three-story manor and wondered if Charlotte was awake. Did she still take a morning ride? Or did she now lay abed and drink chocolate before breaking her fast? Two years ago he couldn't have imagined her staying still for any reason. She was always moving, smiling, laughing. But he didn't know her now like he did then. Maybe she was as changed as he was.

He mounted the steps and walked toward the large wooden door. When they'd been small, David, Charlotte, Marcus and Edward had rarely been so formal as to come through the front door. They'd almost always come through the servants' entrance and pinched sweets from Cook's kitchen. But everything was different now.

Today he would be making arrangements for Charlotte's future. And his own. The one he'd never thought they'd have together.

His heart wanted to rejoice that he would have Charlotte as his wife. But his head knew that theirs could never be a true marriage. He would have to make concessions somehow to protect both of them. It would never do to have Charlotte frightened in her own home because her husband woke screaming, thrashing about in his night terror, and possibly attacking her without realizing.

He straightened his jacket and rapped twice. Farris opened the door a moment later, as if he'd been expecting him, even though it was quite early. "Lord Carlisle." He moved aside and let Edward in. "May I take your hat and coat?"

Edward swept off his hat and handed over his greatcoat. "I'd like to speak with the earl."

"He's waiting for you in his study." Farris pivoted and started down the hall. "I'll escort you there."

Edward matched his pace to the old butler's. Farris's familiar, hunched form calmed Edward's nerves a bit. He'd known Farris since he was a boy running through the halls with David and sliding down the bannister while Charlotte chased them and tried to keep up. Back then, he'd barely noticed the portraits in this hall, but as they walked slowly toward the study, the past generations of Pembroke earls peered down at him, most with a stern and disapproving look on their faces. Edward tugged on his collar and kept his eyes on the butler's back. Charlotte would be well taken care of. No one would have to worry about that. Past or present.

Farris opened the study door and announced him. "Viscount Carlisle, my lord."

Edward walked into the room and David stood up from behind his desk. "Edward, come in. Somehow, I knew you'd want to settle this as soon as the sun was up. You always were an early riser."

He motioned toward the chair in front of his desk and Edward sat. The old earl's study had always been one in which his children were welcome. There was a low table for a tea tray and comfortable chairs if David or Charlotte had wanted to be near while their father worked on estate business. There were also books on the shelves behind the desk that would appeal to all interests. Edward had always been quite envious of David and Charlotte's relationship with their father. He may have been unlucky at the gaming tables, but he'd loved his children and shown it.

Forcing himself to relax, Edward concentrated on the task at hand. He leaned back into the chair and let the warmth of the fire in the grate steal over him. "I'm here to discuss the marriage settlements."

David steepled his hands on his desk. "I'd like to discuss another matter first." He took a breath, as if he truly didn't want to discuss it, but had no choice. "The last time we spoke, you were adamant that the betrothal between you and Charlotte be broken, even going so far as to buy up my vowels and hold them over me." He coughed into his hand. "Since you've returned from the Peninsula, you've not been yourself."

Edward's jaw clenched. This was the conversation he'd hoped to avoid.

David met Edward's eyes. "I feel it my duty as the head of the Pembroke family to tell you that if you can't comport yourself as a faithful, loving husband, then I want to break the betrothal as you outlined previously. I won't see Charlotte hurt or shackled to a lush."

Edward flexed his fingers, tamping down the anger that rose in him at the accusatory tone. "I should call you out for that, but I understand that your words are out of concern for Charlotte."

He leaned forward, suddenly wishing for that closeness he'd once had with David. There had been a time when David had looked at Edward as a man worthy of his sister. "You have my word of honor that I will do my best to make sure Charlotte is the happiest of women as the new Viscountess of Carlisle. I will be a faithful husband and will not embarrass her in any way, and she'll have the respect she deserves for someone of her station."

David shook his head. "You know she doesn't care a fig for titles and protocol. She has loved you for as long as I can remember and has only ever wanted a home and a family with you. Can you still give her those? Or has the war changed you too much?"

Edward thought back to all the times he'd stolen away to the treehouse with Charlotte and how they'd stared up at the branches. They'd talked of having a dozen children to take on picnics and trips to Town for ices. The dream being that their children would only ever know a father's love and never a father's punishments. "Yes, I can."

Or so he hoped. Sitting there, a possible plan formed in Edward's mind. Since most of his dark thoughts and memories assailed him at night, perhaps he could take Charlotte back to Town and ensconce her at Carlisle House, while he kept his bachelor's apartments. Then, after spending the day with her, he could retreat to his apartment in the evening to fight his night demons alone.

"I know I haven't been myself lately, but being at Hartwell has helped me. You don't have to worry about Charlotte," he assured David. And repeated the words silently to himself. If he could only keep some distance from her, he could see to her happiness as his wife and still keep her safe. It wouldn't be quite the same marriage as they'd planned, but perhaps close enough.

"What do you plan to do about my vowels?" For the first time in their discussion, David's voice wavered. Ah. So he wasn't as sure of himself as he appeared.

Edward folded his arms and eyed him across the desk. "I haven't decided as yet, but I do want to make sure that you don't go to the tables ever again."

David let out a long breath. "You don't have to worry about that. I've learned my lesson."

"Whatever possessed you to wager so much when your estate needs every bit to restore it after your father's poor judgment?" Edward sat back again, wanting to hear the answer to the question he hadn't asked before now. "I thought you had learned the lesson well as a lad from watching your father fall so close to ruin."

David's shoulders sagged. "I thought so as well, but the gaming tables are a seductive illusion. When I won a bit of coin, it felt like I'd hit a lucky streak, so I kept going. The lucky streak didn't."

There was deep regret in David's eyes, and Edward felt pity for the man. "You put your family at risk, David. You could have lost everything."

"I know. But I vow that will never happen again." He stood and came around the desk, leaning his hip against the corner.

"Perhaps I shall give them to you as a wedding gift, then." He stood as well. "I want to apologize for my behavior to you these past months. You've been like a brother to me and I've treated you poorly."

David inclined his head. "Thank you for that. The last months have been difficult for all of us. My mother and sister have suffered financially from my poor judgments, as well as having our good name besmirched by the suspicion that I was linked to a possible murder. Though I was cleared of any wrongdoing, the damage had been done among the tabbies of the *ton*. Charlotte has been hurt by those she thought were her friends, and I don't want to see her hurt by you."

Edward stilled. The thought of Charlotte hurt fueled all his protective instincts. "I would never hurt her, and I will stand against anyone who dares to malign Charlotte or her reputation."

"Good." An easiness settled between the two men. David stepped forward to stand next to Edward, as if the formality between them was over. "So we'll call the banns and set the wedding for a month from today." David straightened, as if a burden had been lifted from his shoulders. "The marriage settlements were generous, so I didn't think there needed to be any changes. Did you?"

"No. From what I recall everything was in order. I just hadn't looked them over recently. But if you feel the arrangements are suitable, I'll send them to my solicitor." Edward stood. "I only want to protect Charlotte. Do you understand?"

"More than you know." David shifted his weight from foot to foot, rubbing his hand across his jaw. "I did want to mention something to you. Several of my acquaintances have come home from the war and joined a Veterans Club that Lord Wolverton has organized. He declares that this club is to be an extension of the brotherhood men found on the battlefield. And since you've served, you might enjoy that. When you're back in London, of course."

Edward nodded. He'd served under Christian Wolverton. He was a good man and had been a competent commander in the field. "Thank you. I'll look into it when Charlotte and I return to Town."

David's mouth turned down into a frown. "Will you stay at Hartwell for the holidays? I know my mother would love to have her children here for the Christmas season."

His mother would, too. "I'll discuss it with Charlotte." Edward reached out and shook David's hand. "Thank you for your understanding about my . . . ailments."

"And thank you for understanding about my misjudgment at the gaming tables. I will pay my debt to you and buy my vowels back. It might take some time, but I consider it a matter of honor." David clapped Edward on the back, his mouth quirked in a half-smile. "I'm glad to see the Edward I know and remember before me."

"It's good to be home." Edward could vaguely recall the few times he'd met David while in London. He'd mostly been foxed or well on his way. It did feel good to be sober and in familiar company.

They walked to the front hall, discussing the drainage ditch that bordered both their properties and needed attention. Neither of them noticed the woman at the top of the stairs until she started toward them, her heels clicking on the polished wood as she descended.

"How very providential to see you today, Lord Carlisle. We have much to discuss," Charlotte said.

Edward watched her approach, remembering all the times he'd dreamed of her just as she was right now—wearing a blue dress that matched her eyes, the corners of her mouth tilting up in a small smile just for him. He bowed. "My lady. I'm happy to discuss anything you like."

"Shall we take a turn about the gardens?" She took Edward's arm without waiting for his reply.

Edward met David's eyes and inclined his head. "If your brother permits, of course."

David waved his hand. "Yes, yes. And I'll talk to my steward about your ideas for a ditch that would better drain. I might have to consult with you further on it, though."

"It would be my pleasure." Edward and Charlotte took their leave in the direction of the terrace doors that led to the garden. Her steps were brisk as they walked down the hall. "Are we in a hurry?" he asked, amused that she seemed anxious to be alone with him.

He felt lighter. His conversation with David had gone well, and with Charlotte by his side, he was starting to believe that perhaps they really could have a marriage. He would just need to stay away from her in the evening hours. And during all thunderstorms.

"I have a matter of utmost importance to discuss with you," she said, her tone solemn, her steps slowing.

"Is it about your trousseau? Perhaps whether I have a proper wedding suit?" He teased. Happiness and teasing seemed almost foreign now, but the feelings were coming back to him. He'd missed letting in any sunshine to relieve the gloom he'd been living.

She turned, unsmiling, to face him and took a deep breath. She clasped her hands together and met his gaze head on. "No, Edward. I need to tell you that I can't marry you. Not now. Perhaps not ever."

CHAPTER 10

harlotte moved away, her fingers twisting in the folds of her dress, unable to bear the hurt look on Edward's face. "I'm sorry," she murmured. "I don't mean to cause you any distress."

"Distress?" He sounded dazed, and the happiness Charlotte had seen earlier as he spoke with David was surely gone now. He cleared his throat. "You've just informed me that you won't marry me. That's a bit more than distressing."

"I know." She wanted desperately to explain, but couldn't seem to find the words. How could she tell him so he'd understand?

"What is it, then?" His voice had hardened to the tone she'd heard most since he'd come home. "We've been betrothed for years. Everyone expects it."

"That's just it." She turned to look at him finally and resisted the urge to wring her hands. Instead, she clasped them together. "I don't want to marry just because everyone expects it."

His familiar brown eyes searched hers as they faced each other. "I know that's not all. Tell me the truth."

She raised her chin. If he wanted the truth, she'd give it to him. "You've wanted to break our betrothal since you returned. You've mentioned several times that you don't wish to marry, and I won't marry someone whose hand is being forced."

He rubbed a hand over his jaw and glanced away. "Charlotte, we were caught in an embrace. We must marry. The marriage contracts are in place, and your brother has given his permission."

"My reputation has suffered already this year. Surely another scandal won't matter when the damage is done." She shrugged, but the fact of the matter was, those cuts had hurt.

"I won't be the cause of tarnish to your reputation or for you to be the topic of gossip. And anyone who slights you will deal with me." His mouth drew into a firm line as if he were getting ready to jump to her defense.

Ah. Her champion. She gave him a grateful smile. "Thank you for that assurance. But my reputation aside, *I* haven't accepted any proposals."

They reached the stone bench on the far side of the nearly bare garden. The bench was still visible from the house, but did offer a bit of privacy. She sat and arranged her skirts. Edward sat next to her, a bit too close for propriety's sake. Charlotte scooted away, putting some distance between them.

"You accepted my proposal before I left for the war." His voice was quiet, but warm. Was he remembering that moment as she did? He'd kissed her when she'd said yes, his lips soft and possessive. The memory of that kiss had gotten her through many lonely nights while he was at war.

"You said it yourself, the war changed you." She let out a sigh. "Edward, we're just getting to know each other again. Let's not confuse the issue with a forced marriage."

"So, your feelings for me haven't changed?" He nudged her chin upward with his knuckles, and when their eyes met, he ran his thumb over her cheek. At his touch, tingles ran down her spine and she leaned in, unable to stop herself. No matter what, she would always want this man by her side.

"No, my feelings haven't changed, but *we've* changed. And we need to get to know one another again." She pressed her cheek to his palm. "I want a true marriage with you, one full of love, laughter, and happiness, with all the children our arms can hold. But I can't marry you if you don't feel like we can have that now."

"What are you suggesting, then?" He'd inched so close to her; she could feel his body heat. Oh how she wished he would put his arms around her. But she had to tell him what she'd decided after the ball last night. It was the only plan that made sense.

"Let's take the time for a proper courtship. At least through the holidays. If, at the end of that time, we find we don't suit, we'll break the betrothal." She leaned away to add weight to her words and separate her emotions from what needed to be said.

"And if we find that we do suit?" His voice was so soft and the question hung in the air. Did he want to stay with her? Oh, how her heart longed for that.

"Then we'll marry as we've always planned." She bit her lip and squared her shoulders. That's all she'd thought of for so long. Being married to him was the outcome she hoped for but worried she'd never have. "But we need to make sure that's what we both want."

"I appreciate your approach." Edward stood. "And I agree. You deserve a proper courtship." He bowed and took her hand, pressing a kiss to the back of it. "We'll start this afternoon. Lady Charlotte, would you accompany me on a drive after luncheon?"

Charlotte smiled at his formality and looked up at his dear and earnest face. "I'd be delighted." She stood and looped her arm through his. "Where shall we drive to?"

"Hmm..." He put his hand on his chin, as if he was thinking

hard. "I've never courted a lady before. Where do courting couples go?"

"I've never been courted before, so I'm not sure, either. We could drive out to the old abbey ruins." She looked up at the blue sky with only a few wispy clouds. "It doesn't look like it's going to be bad weather, but with the English countryside, you can never be quite sure. Although, a good cloak could guard against any chill."

"I'm sure we would be able to stay warm." There was a teasing glint in Edward's eye and Charlotte felt a flush climb her neck. His kisses would also warm her, but she would never dare say that out loud.

He grinned, as if he could read her thoughts. "You know we've both seen the abbey ruins so many times, we could probably draw a map of them blindfolded." Edward shook his head as they resumed their leisurely stroll through the once fragrant gardens that were now awaiting winter. "But since I don't have a better suggestion, the abbey ruins it is."

"Maybe it will look different since you haven't seen it for quite a while," she said, squeezing his arm. A breeze flitted over them, as if spiriting away any gloom from earlier. "And I could bring a hamper from Cook. That should lift your spirits."

He did seem to brighten at that. "Perhaps that would help," he agreed. "And we could bring the dog, as well. That could add an element of adventure. She loves a good romp."

"Have you been keeping company with her, then?" Charlotte looked at him, curious to know the answer. He had a soft spot in his heart for animals, but she couldn't recall him ever having a personal pet.

"Yes. She's actually quite a good listener until she spots a rabbit or anything else she can chase." He smiled at her ruefully. "Unless that's just a ruse and I've bored the poor dog silly so she runs off."

"I'm certain her manners would be better than that. She must be feeling more the thing, then." It warmed Charlotte's heart to think of Edward and the dog together. Perhaps their two wounded souls needed each other.

"Yes, she seems to be in fine form. And Mrs. Blackhurst spoils her with bones and scraps."

"She needed a bit of spoiling." *Like Edward did*, Charlotte thought. "I'd love to renew my acquaintance with her."

"I'll invite her along on our outing then." Edward seemed pleased with himself, and that pleased Charlotte.

They reached the house and he held the door for her. Charlotte reluctantly let go of his arm and stepped through. He reached for her again as soon as they gained the hall, however, and she smiled, happy that he wanted to be close. She'd missed his touch since he'd been home.

The butler was waiting for them at the door and immediately produced Edward's coat and hat. Charlotte had wanted to prolong Edward's call with the offer of tea, but now she had an outing to look forward to.

"I'll return for you directly after luncheon," Edward said as he put on his hat. "Don't forget the hamper."

Charlotte smothered a laugh. "I won't. And I'll see if our Cook has a bone or other treat for our furry friend. Perhaps our kitchen scraps compare to Hartwell's."

"We won't tell Mrs. Blackhurst of the competition. It might prick her sensitivities, and she would feel obligated to provide the best scraps, and then the dog would be more than spoiled by two houses." Edward took her hand once more and held it to his heart. "Until this afternoon, my lady."

Charlotte inclined her head and watched him take his leave. His words sent a thrill through her, for she truly did want to be his lady. But only if they could share in the love that had been between them and perhaps have a chance to live the life they'd once dreamed of as husband and wife.

She turned to go upstairs and decide which gown she'd wear for their outing. Her spirit had been heavy when she'd anticipated talking with Edward this morning, but now she felt as if she could float away with happiness. He'd understood. And even though she knew this courtship might yet end in heartbreak, for the moment, she let hope blossom in her chest. No matter what happened, the memory of his smile and gentle touch would be something she treasured forever.

CHAPTER 11

*E*dward couldn't seem to sit still. He'd paced the length of his study, going from the window to the desk. He was nervous. Though he'd been to the abbey ruins with Charlotte thousands of times as children, and even after they'd grown up, this would be their first time to be there as part of an official courtship.

He eyed the brandy in the snifter behind the desk and shook his head. No, he didn't need any liquid courage today. This was Charlotte. She knew him as well as he knew himself. There was nothing to be nervous about.

He straightened his cravat, then moved toward the door to call for the carriage to be brought around. Before he could touch the handle, a light rap sounded on the other side. Opening it, his butler, Simmons, was standing in the hall.

"My lord," he said, pulling back slightly. "I didn't expect you to open the door so quickly . . . I'm sorry if I've disturbed you."

"What is it, Simmons?" Edward asked as he walked past him and started down the hall. "I need the carriage brought around immediately. I don't want to be late to appear on Lady Charlotte's doorstep. That wouldn't leave a good impression."

"My lord." Simmons picked up his pace and matched strides with Edward. "You have a caller. A Lord Wolverton."

Edward stopped, and his heart skipped a beat. There was no reason for Lord Wolverton to come down from London to visit him and Hartwell Manor was too far out of the way to be a stopping place. Did he have bad news of some sort? "Lord Wolverton? Here?"

"Yes, my lord. I put him in the drawing room and called for a tea tray to be sent up." Simmons looked pleased with himself.

Edward scowled. Whatever Wolverton's business was, he wanted the interview over with quickly. "I don't have time for a tea tray. I won't be late for my appointment with Lady Charlotte."

Simmons dipped his head. "Yes, my lord. I shall inform the cook."

Edward gave a great sigh. Wolverton had probably traveled most of the afternoon and would be hungry. "No, send the tea tray in."

Once Simmons had gone, Edward turned on his heel and marched toward the drawing room, feeling for all the world like he was back in Spain being called to his superior officer's quarters. Wolverton had been his captain, and they'd fought side by side together through more battles than Edward cared to count. But what was he doing here?

Opening the door to the drawing room, he entered and immediately closed it behind him. His servants were discreet, but Edward didn't know what this call would be about. If it had to do with the war, Spain, or anything that had happened there, he wanted complete privacy. No one could know what he'd endured or how it had affected him.

Wolverton had drawn back the drapes and was standing near

the windows that overlooked the estate's tree-lined drive. He seemed to be staring at the trees, which were without even one leaf, leaving the branches naked and shivering in the chill wind.

Wolverton turned at his entrance. "Edward. I apologize for having drawn back the drapes when I know the house is in mourning, but I'm afraid dark, enclosed rooms can be difficult for me."

Edward was surprised at the admission. "Because of what happened at the church?" he asked softly. The doors had been shut on the dying and wounded through that long, horrible night. The darkness and cramped quarters had been enough to scar the souls of men like Edward and Wolverton who had been there attempting to comfort and help.

"Partly, yes. I find that light and open spaces helps to remind me I'm in England now. When there is light, that is," he said with a small smile. "English weather often doesn't cooperate with my wishes."

Edward joined him at the window. Looking into his former commanding officer's face brought back so many memories---not all of them bad. There had been laughter and camaraderie as well as horror and pain, fear and loss.

"To what do I owe this pleasure?" he asked. A slow shiver of unease was making its way up his spine.

"Can we sit?" Wolverton moved toward the chairs behind them and sat down in the nearest one. Edward sat to his right, trying to look composed. "I've been worried about you since I saw you at the Huntington ball," Wolverton said quietly. "You didn't appear to have adjusted to civilian life very well."

"I'm managing," Edward said. "It has been easier for me to cope at our country seat with my mother." *And Charlotte*, he silently added.

"I was sorry to hear about your father." Wolverton watched him closely. "And I don't want to disturb you while you're in mourning, but this couldn't wait."

"What is it?" He stilled his tapping foot. His shoulders were tense and nervous energy was rushing through Edward's veins. He stood to stir up the fire a little more. Wolverton sounded so serious. This must have something to do with the war, that's the only thing he could imagine. Edward wanted to pace, but forced himself back to his chair. Wolverton waited until he'd taken his seat again.

"Though the war has ended, I still keep in touch with a few of my French informants. They were a great help to me while we were in Spain, and wish to keep the peace as much as we do. But I recently got a message from one of them that I thought would be of interest to you." Wolverton's eyes met his, searching.

Edward furrowed his brow and swallowed. "What did it say?"

He leaned forward in his seat. "I have reason to believe that Marcus survived and is being held captive by a French lieutenant."

Edward felt as if the air had been sucked from the room. There was a roaring in his head. The words were still echoing through his mind, *"Marcus survived."* But how could that be? Edward had held his hand until no more breath had come from his body. Then he'd been forced to march away and leave him behind without a burial. Marcus's wounds had been fatal.

"I can't believe it," Edward finally said, shaking his head. "It can't be true. I was there when Marcus breathed his last."

Wolverton bowed his head, then raised it to look at Edward. "I have to know if there is even the smallest chance that this intelligence is true. If Marcus is indeed being held prisoner, I want to do all I can to free him."

The thought of Marcus as a prisoner to the French soured Edward's stomach. Dying might have been better than to have faced that. "You're right, of course. I want to go with you and see it through." Did he dare hope that Marcus was still alive?

"I don't think that's the best course of action." Wolverton's voice was gentle, as if he wasn't sure how Edward would react. "I just wanted you to be informed. I have never had cause to doubt this informant's word before, and I know Marcus was your best friend."

Edward shook his head and stood, lurching toward the windows, needing air, but knowing he had to stay in this room and hear the rest of it. "Please. You must let me help you. I . . . I was supposed to protect Marcus. I've not been able to forgive myself for his death. And now if he's been held prisoner all these months . . ." He ran a hand through his hair. Was that worse? To be alive, but a prisoner?

Wolverton trailed in his footsteps and set a hand on Edward's shoulder. "If I did consider allowing you to accompany me, I need to know you can keep your head about you. No matter what we find."

Edward clenched his fists. He had to go with Wolverton to find out Marcus's fate. "I'll do anything you need. Please, tell me what to do."

Wolverton nodded. "If you're certain, then I'll need you to come back to London. I'm to wait there for the next missive. There is a chance we may have to travel to France." Wolverton put his hands behind his back, but kept his eyes on Edward. "Would you be prepared to go back to a country ravaged by war? It's possible that might prove too difficult for you, especially when you've just returned home and are finding your way again. I don't want to be the cause of you taking a step backward when I know you've struggled."

It would be very difficult, but Edward wouldn't say that aloud. "You can depend on me, Captain." Edward felt the flush rising on his neck at the idea that Wolverton seemed to think him so weak. He wanted to prove him wrong. "I'm betrothed to Lady Charlotte, and we are to be married in four weeks. Would we be back in time?"

Charlotte. How was he going to explain this to her? She'd allowed him a chance to court her and win her again. Leaving for France before their wedding wouldn't put much confidence in her heart, especially after all they'd been through since his return to Hartwell. Could he make her understand? Would she consider marrying him without the promised courtship? He hated asking it of her.

"I'm not sure when we would return. It depends on what we discover and how far we have to go to find him. And I'm afraid I must ask you not to mention that Marcus may be alive to anyone other than your mother and your betrothed and to put them under strict confidence. The hope of Marcus being alive would hardly be fair to his family if it turns out to be an unfortunate mistake, and news like that would travel quickly. But I know the women will worry if you disappear without any word." Wolverton gave him an apologetic look.

Edward nodded. Having to lie to his mother or Charlotte would have been difficult, and Charlotte might not have forgiven him. At least he had permission to share this confidence with her. "I'm to see her this afternoon and will explain then."

Wolverton turned as the door opened and the tea tray was brought in. The maid set it down near Edward and quickly withdrew. Edward handed a plate to Wolverton, who helped himself to several biscuits.

"You know, perhaps if Lady Charlotte doesn't object, you could move the wedding up by several weeks and bring her with you to London. It might be better to have her at your side while we wait for news and decide the best way to find Marcus." Wolverton watched him as he bit into the biscuit. He chewed and swallowed before adding, "Would she be amenable to something like that?"

"I believe so." But he didn't know. Edward's stomach twisted. He'd promised to court Charlotte and woo her as she deserved so they could get to know one another. He wanted that. He wanted her to be his wife and couldn't imagine asking her to wait for him again. But he didn't know if she would consider moving up the wedding without the courtship. Perhaps she would if he laid his heart before her and showed he was the man she'd always known and trusted.

But would doing so be enough?

He was about to find out. Taking a deep breath, he met Wolverton's eyes. "My wife and I will meet you in London in two days' time."

And he hoped that statement to be true.

CHAPTER 12

Charlotte sat in the parlor, trying not to watch for a carriage coming down the drive. Edward was late and she was starting to wonder if he was really coming. Cook had delivered the hamper nearly an hour before. And Charlotte had already checked with Farris—there had been no note from Hartwell.

She sighed. Had he changed his mind? Had something happened? Standing up to pace again, she turned when the door opened.

"He better have a good reason for keeping you waiting," David said as he came into the room.

"I'm sure he does." She looked back toward the window. He'd been sincere this morning in wanting to court her. She was sure of that. "I hope something hasn't happened to him."

"Shall I go out in search of him?" David inclined his head toward her, a protective older brother tone in his voice. "I'm happy to run him to ground for you."

Charlotte immediately declined the offer. "That won't be necessary. I'm sure he'll be here momentarily."

David motioned her to the sofa, and she sat. He took the seat next to her and picked up her hand. "I asked him if he could be a good and faithful husband to you, Charlie. He said he could and would." He looked into her eyes. "But is he what you still want? If you've decided he's changed too much, there is still time to cry off."

"You are such a dear brother." Charlotte squeezed his fingers. "Edward is the only man I will ever love. I have no doubt he'll be the best of husbands. But thank you for looking out for me."

The sounds of a carriage coming down the drive reached her ears, and she jumped up. "He's here." Her voice was tinged with relief. He hadn't changed his mind.

David smiled at her indulgently. "Will you wait in here for him to collect you? Or shall we meet him at the door?"

Charlotte retook her seat. "Don't be silly. We'll wait in here," she said, primly.

Edward was ushered into the room, and it was easy to see that something was heavy on his mind. His jaw was clenched as he bowed to Charlotte. "Please pardon my tardiness," he said, his tone formal. "It could not be helped."

Charlotte's heart sank. They'd only been apart for mere hours, and yet she could see by his demeanor that he was deeply troubled.

"Is everything all right, Carlisle?" David asked, a frown furrowing his brow.

"I need to speak to Charlotte." Edward couldn't take his eyes off of her, which made Charlotte's nervousness come back in full force.

Perhaps he had changed his mind after all.

Charlotte slowly drew in a breath. "Of course. Would you still like to go to the ruins or would you prefer to speak here?" Whatever he had to say, she would bear it. If he'd truly come to break their betrothal, she wouldn't beg or cry.

"Could we speak here?" Edward looked around and his gaze came back to Charlotte. "Time is of the essence."

"Listen here, Carlisle, if something has happened that involves my sister, I should be aware of it as well." David puffed out his chest. "We should all hear what you have to say."

Charlotte shook her head. Edward wanted privacy to inform her of his news. Her brother's protective instincts would make it that much harder. "David, please excuse us. If there is anything you should be made aware of, we'll come to your study."

David gave her a disgruntled frown, but moved toward the door. "I'd like to speak with you after Carlisle is gone," he said before he went through the doorway.

"Very well." Charlotte gave an impatient sigh as he didn't quite close the door, leaving it a bit ajar, as was proper. Right now she wished for complete privacy, though. Every muscle in Edward's body seemed tense. She tried to steel herself for whatever Edward was about to say. It definitely wasn't going to be good news.

"Won't you sit?" she invited, motioning toward the seat next to her on the sofa.

He sat, but only on the edge of the cushion with his knee bouncing in an excited rhythm, as if he couldn't stop moving and was anxious to stand once again.

"Whatever is the matter, Edward?" she asked quietly. "Is your mother well?"

"Yes, yes, she's in fine form." He ran his hands through his hair. He was obviously quite distracted. "Something extraordinary has happened."

She reached for his hand. He felt very far away and she wanted to pull him to her. "What is it?"

He turned to face her more fully. "I've had news from my

former commanding officer. There is a possibility that Marcus is still alive." He swallowed. 'He may be a captive of a French lieutenant."

Charlotte gasped and put her hand to her mouth. "Alive?" The world seemed to tilt as she took in what he'd said. She'd been devastated by Marcus's loss. Could it be true that he hadn't died?

Edward took her other hand in his. "Even if there is the smallest chance of this being true, I must try to find out."

"I . . . I can't believe it." Charlotte's mind was spinning for what this could mean for Marcus's father. Everyone who loved him.

"I can hardly believe it myself." Edward's voice was full of wonder. "I can't tell you what it would mean to have him back. I can hardly think of anything but going to find him."

"You're leaving." It wasn't a question. Of course he was. Her heart sank. They'd just started to find their footing again. "When?"

"Tomorrow." He shifted closer to her. "Charlotte, the last time I left I asked you to wait for me. This time I'd like to ask you to come with me." He knelt in front of her and kept her hand in his. "Charlotte, will you do me the great honor of becoming my wife? Tomorrow?"

Her heart turned over in her chest. He wanted her with him. She wouldn't have to wait for him and she rejoiced in that fact. "Yes," she said simply. If he was going to leave, she wanted to be by his side. She'd wanted to be courted, to know him again, but perhaps the fates were telling her she'd have to trust that the bond they'd already built would be a good foundation for their marriage.

Edward kissed her forehead and rose to his feet. "Apparently, my father had procured a special license for us, hoping that I would come home before he died, and he could witness our marriage." His countenance dimmed, but he continued on. "The license is still valid, so we can wed in the morning." He looked down into her face, searching her eyes. "Are you sure a marriage in haste will suit you? I know you wanted to have a courtship before we wed."

His brows drew down in concern, and she wanted to smooth away his worries. "I would much rather be with you as your wife then wait and wonder if you will come home to me. And if we can find Marcus alive? Then it would be a miracle." One they could experience together. "Your family is in mourning, Edward. What did your mother say when you told her of your plans?"

"She'd been hoping for the match all along, so she was quite happy. Of course, with her being in mourning, it wouldn't be seemly for more than immediate family to attend the ceremony." Edward still looked concerned. "I'm sorry, Charlie. I know you had grand plans for your wedding day."

"Much has changed over the last two years." Since her return from London and the rumormongers there, she'd be perfectly content with only her family and Edward's as witnesses. "An intimate family wedding suits me just fine."

"Can you be at the Hartwell chapel at nine tomorrow morning?" A smile curved his lips, and her heart skipped a beat. This was the Edward she'd always known. Kind, caring, sweet Edward.

"Yes." Happiness and nervousness bubbled up inside her. She would be Edward's wife. Tomorrow. And they would set out to find Marcus. Together. It seemed a dream. A wonderful dream. "I'll be ready."

He looked down at her and reached out a hand to caress her cheek. "I don't know what I've done to deserve you," he said, his voice low. "But I never want you to be sorry you agreed to be my wife."

"I won't." Charlotte lifted her chin. Would he kiss her as he had when he'd proposed years ago? He was standing so close, his breath mingled with hers. His eyes dipped to her lips, and she wet them with her tongue. The air around them seemed charged with electricity, and she leaned in even closer, placing her hands on his chest. "Edward."

He bent, and her eyes fluttered closed. When his lips brushed her cheek, however, she opened her eyes again. His heart was beating as hard as hers under her hand, and the look in his eyes sent warmth from her head to her toes.

"Until tomorrow then," he said, stepping back and taking an unsteady breath.

She hid her stab of disappointment that he hadn't kissed her. Perhaps he was waiting until their wedding ceremony. That must be it. Inhaling, she put on a bright smile. "Yes. I'll see you in the morning."

And by the afternoon, she wouldn't have to wait for Edward's kisses ever again or wonder if he would come home. He would be hers.

Tomorrow couldn't come soon enough.

CHAPTER 13

*E*dward stood at the front of the chapel, a trickle of sweat beading on his brow. He took a deep breath and let it out slowly. He was marrying Charlotte today. Even though there was so much to consider when he returned to London to help Wolverton find Marcus, today, he wanted only to think of Charlotte.

The door at the back opened, and Charlotte entered on her brother's arm. Edward caught his breath at her beauty. She wore a sky-blue gown just darker than her eyes, with a little bit of white lacy trim at the bodice. Her hair was swept up, leaving her neck bare but for her mother's pearl necklace around her throat. Her eyes met his, and her mouth curved in a wide smile and his heart seemed to calm. Their wedding wasn't what they'd planned in their youth—when times were simpler and he'd believed love could conquer all—but she was here. Smiling. And about to become his wife.

Her brother walked her slowly down the aisle, and the thought crossed Edward's mind that perhaps he still hadn't won David's blessing. Had he reassured David sufficiently that he would be a good husband to Charlotte? Even with the secrets he still held, Charlotte owned his heart. She always had. Surely David knew that.

For a fleeting second Edward regretted not giving Charlotte the special day she deserved. The pews should have been filled with all of London's elite, but instead, only their mothers, Wolverton and David were there. The old feelings of inadequacy started to creep into his heart.

But his eyes caught Charlotte's again, and she gave him a small nod. It was as if she'd read his mind and was letting him know everything was fine. He was all right. Relaxing his shoulders, he reached for her as she approached. "My lady," he murmured.

Her hand was cold as he squeezed her fingers. Was she nervous? He turned to face her and took both of her hands in his, glad to finally be able to touch her and have her close. Her cheeks were pink, as if a blush had kissed her skin and left only a dainty glow behind. The light of her smile overshadowed anything else, and he returned it. She was about to become his wife. How could he be anything but happy?

The vicar began the ceremony, but Edward hardly heard a word. He kept his gaze on Charlotte, all the memories of her running through his head. How she'd stubbornly followed after him, Marcus, and David on their adventures. How she'd turned into a young woman seemingly overnight and turned his head at the same time. How happy he'd been to know she loved him as he loved her. The wrenching goodbye when he'd gone off to war and his promise to come back for her and be her husband.

And now he would be.

She was looking up at him with trust shining in her eyes. Edward wanted to live up to that. He wasn't the man she'd known, and he didn't want to disappoint her. In the short time he'd been home, however, he now knew he couldn't live without her. To want her by his side was selfish when he was still struggling with the demons he'd brought home with him. Yet the stars had aligned their fates so that no matter what he did, it seemed they would be together. It was time he accepted that.

The vicar had stopped talking and was staring at him expectantly. "I will," Edward said solemnly.

Charlotte let out a little breath as if she'd been holding it. Had she thought he would leave her at the altar? He stood straighter. No, she wouldn't think that of him. But no matter what, he was going to do everything in his power to be the man she thought him to be. It might not happen right away, but he was determined.

When Charlotte stated her vows, her voice was clear and unwavering. And before he knew it, the ceremony was over and the moment had come to kiss his bride. He looked down at her and inched closer. Her eyes crinkled in a smile, and he touched his lips to hers. She was soft and smelled like lilacs, and he closed his eyes, as if by doing so, he could forget there were guests in the church looking on. He wanted to lose himself in her—in her goodness. When he kissed her, he felt like the man he'd been before he left.

Reluctantly releasing her, he smiled and cupped her shoulders. "Thank you," he said softly.

She let out a low chuckle as she smoothed his cravat. "For what?"

"Being brave enough to become my wife." He slid his palm down her arm and lifted her hand to his lips to gently press a kiss to the back of it.

"Were you worried I might change my mind?" Her eyebrows were raised and, though it was obvious from her playful tone that she was teasing him, a guilty flush rose on his neck as he recalled their conversation when he'd first returned to Hartwell. How had he ever thought that it was a good idea to break their betrothal? If he could take those actions back, he would.

"I've always wanted the best for you, Charlotte. There was a time I thought that wasn't me." Edward wanted her to understand and to have their marriage start with honesty between them.

"You have always been what's best for me, Edward. Always." She squeezed his arm and he took a long breath. She'd never given up on him. It was humbling.

Their mothers approached, both of them dabbing their eyes with their handkerchiefs. The new Viscount and his Viscountess turned to greet their few guests with hugs and felicitations. A wedding luncheon had been planned and prepared at Winslow Hall and once they were through eating, then Edward and Charlotte would go on to a cottage near Edward's estate. They would spend the night there, then travel to London in the morning. Though the wedding had been put together in haste, at least the day promised to be as celebratory as if they'd spent months.

They exited the church to find two carriages waiting for them. When David, Wolverton, and both of their mothers had pulled away in the first carriage, Charlotte and Edward climbed in the second one for the short trip back to the house. Everyone was in a happy mood as Farris directed them to the dining room. They sat down to a great feast that the Pembroke cook had prepared. Edward was quite surprised at the variety of meats, cheeses, soups, jellies, cakes, and biscuits. With such short notice, the kitchen staff must have worked half the night.

Edward was seated next to Charlotte and ate heartily as he watched her. She was so beautiful and happy. Full of light. She stayed by his side, occasionally squeezing his hand as if to make sure he was still there. The longer he stayed in her company, the easier it was to believe that they could make their marriage work. No matter what had happened in the past, he was now Charlotte's husband. She laughed at something her brother said, a genuine sound of happiness. He wanted to hear that for the rest of his life and be the one that elicited the sound.

He was anxious to have her alone.

"Are you ready to go, my dear?" he asked when there was a break in the conversation and she turned to him again.

"Yes." She touched his cheek. "My trunks are loaded in the carriage so we can leave anytime you like."

"Then it's time to say our farewells." He looked around the table at everyone smiling indulgently at them, except for David. He still sported a concerned crease in his brow whenever he looked at Edward. In time, Edward hoped to remove that look permanently from his new brother-in-law's face by proving that Charlotte would be cared for and happy.

Charlotte stood. "Thank you all for a wonderful day. My husband and I," she paused to smile at him, "are going to take our leave."

Charlotte's mother put a handkerchief to her mouth. "So soon?"

"We shall be in London only for a few weeks, Mama, and then we shall be back at Winslow Hall for the holidays." She moved around the table to reassure her mother. Charlotte always seemed to be attuned to others' feelings. With one more assurance that she would do her best to return to Winslow for Christmas, she hugged her mother close.

Edward felt a twinge of regret. It would be such a disappointment for Charlotte if they didn't return for Christmas with her family. So much depended on when they found Marcus and to what lengths they had to go to bring him home. But Charlotte couldn't tell her family that.

While Charlotte was still deep in conversation, Edward's mother went to his side. "I'm so happy for you, and I know your father would be, too." She touched his arm, but Edward had frozen at the mention of his father. He hadn't thought of the man for days and certainly did not want to think of him on his wedding day.

"Thank you, Mother," he said stiffly.

"And I think your dog will miss you greatly, but you're right, London is no place for a dog who likes to roam. Though, she's already tried to get into my bedchamber twice today. Perhaps she's thinking she will keep me warm at night while you are away?" His mother arched a brow.

"She does provide a fair bit of warmth." Edward liked the idea of the dog keeping his mother company. "And we shall do our best to be home for the holidays."

"I was dearly hoping to spend Christmas with my son and his wife this year. I wasn't sure that would even be a possibility at all, yet here we are." His mother gave him a mischievous grin before she sobered, her forehead furrowing. "I know we still have grievances to air before things will truly be easy between us, but not today." Her tone brooked no argument, and he didn't offer one. "I do have one word of advice to give you. Charlotte loves you. Let her love in. Love is the most healing balm in all the world."

And with that, she moved away. Edward watched her go. He hoped he could take her advice. He wanted to.

David waved to him from the far corner of the room and motioned toward the hall. Charlotte was still talking to her mother, so Edward let out a sigh and followed.

"David." Edward said, as he walked into the corridor. "What do you want to speak to me about?"

David clasped his hands behind his back but got straight to the point. "I know the settlements have been signed and everything is in writing, but beyond my sister being taken care of monetarily, I want to impress upon you how important Charlotte's happiness is to me." He leaned in and let out a deep breath, his gaze set on

Edward. "To be clear, if you don't do everything in your power to be the husband she deserves, I will call you out."

Edward looked at the man in front of him, who had been one of his two best friends in the world. David, Marcus, and Edward. They'd been inseparable. Edward wished for the innocence of those days once again. He'd thought all was lost when Marcus died, that those old memories would be all he had when he thought of their trio of friends. Yet, if he were alive and Edward could help bring him home, the three of them could make new memories. The future seemed so much brighter. How he wished he could confide in David that Marcus might be alive. David had loved him as much as Edward had.

"As I said before, I will do everything possible to assure her happiness." Or he would die trying.

David nodded as Charlotte joined them in the hall. "What's this?" she asked, looking between the two men. "Surely you can't be having a row on my wedding day."

"Just saying our goodbyes," David said as he kissed her on the forehead. "Be happy, dearest." He reached out and shook Edward's hand. "Send word when you reach London."

"I will," Edward said as he escorted Charlotte to the front door. Farris handed Edward his coat and Charlotte her cloak. Once they were ready, he opened the door. They started down the steps to the waiting carriage. Before Edward could hand Charlotte in, a horse came around the corner from the direction of the stable. Edward shaded his eyes. It was Wolverton who dismounted before he approached. They met him on the drive, just far enough away from the coachman that they could speak privately.

"May I offer you both my congratulations," he said, as he took off his hat. "Thank you for allowing me to witness your nuptials."

"You're welcome," Charlotte said with a smile. "It was so good of you to agree."

"It was my pleasure." Wolverton bowed. "I'll be heading back to London today. Lord Carlisle, I'll contact you in two days' time to talk about our next steps." He put his hand on Edward's shoulder. "We'll find him."

Edward had no doubt of that. "Yes, we will."

Wolverton put his hat back on and mounted his horse. Charlotte and Edward watched him go down the long drive that led from the house.

"He was a good soldier, wasn't he?" Charlotte asked.

"One of the best." They walked back to the carriage and Edward handed her in and then settled himself next to his wife.

His wife. He would never get tired of thinking of her like that.

As the carriage moved forward and the house disappeared behind them, Charlotte watched out the window until it was a tiny speck, as if she could hardly bear to leave Winslow Hall. Did she have misgivings already?

Edward clasped his hands together. He had to know. "Any regrets?"

Charlotte looked up at him and laughed lightly. "None at all. I confess, I'm a trifle nervous about returning to London. I had a hard time of it when I was there last Season." She moved closer to him on the seat and let her head rest on his shoulder. "But I know I don't have to worry as long as you are by my side."

Edward put his arm around her and drew her close to him. "You don't have to worry one bit." He kissed the top of her head. "I'll keep you safe."

"I love you, Edward." She didn't look up at him or seem to expect a reply. His stomach twisted. He wanted to say it to her. But he couldn't. Not just yet. He had a few more dragons to slay before he could say it out loud and feel like he could give her his whole self---body, heart, and soul.

So why did it feel as if he'd failed her already? "Charlotte."

She leaned in and put two fingers on his lips. "I know we have a long road to travel, and you don't feel the same way about me as you once did. But we were best friends before the war, and we can be again. I know it. And I'm willing to wait until you remember who you were when we were together."

His heart cracked open just a bit at her words. He didn't deserve her, but was so grateful to have her. He looked down into her face, the sun slanting through the window and highlighting her hair around her head like a halo. *Angelic*, he decided.

"I will always be your friend, Charlotte. You can count on that." He kissed her forehead and they settled back in the seats. Perhaps he was getting a chance to atone for the mistakes he'd made. He could find Marcus and be the man Charlotte thought him to be. Maybe then he could forgive himself for that one day when everything he'd ever known seemed to upend itself and hadn't ever been righted. With Charlotte in his arms, he felt as if he could repair it all somehow and have the life he'd once dreamed of.

And if this was his chance, he was going to make sure he didn't waste it.

CHAPTER 14

Charlotte took a deep breath and opened her eyes. The gentle swaying of the carriage had stopped. As the events of the morning came back to her, she realized her cheek was pillowed on Edward's chest and his arm held her securely to his side. She was loath to move. It felt too good to be in his embrace.

"We're here," Edward said, brushing some hair from her face. "Are you awake?"

"Yes." She sat up slowly and looked out the window. Dark clouds had moved in, but the sun was valiantly trying to shine through onto the house. "What a lovely cottage." It was a smaller manor house, with a symmetrical façade and box sash windows. Rosebushes lined the walk in front of it.

"I'm glad you like it." The carriage door opened and John Coachman put down the steps. Edward got out and reached back to take her hand. She slipped her fingers into his and alighted from the carriage. Edward's eyes scanned the sky, frowning at the charcoal-colored clouds. Was he worried about a little rain on their wedding day?

He put her hand on his arm and turned just as an older gentleman opened the door of the cottage. "We've been expecting you, Lord Carlisle," the man said with a bow.

Edward inclined his head. "It's good to see you, Banks." An older woman joined Banks at the door, and Edward leaned toward Charlotte. "Lady Carlisle, these are the caretakers of Rose Cottage, Mr. and Mrs. Banks."

Charlotte couldn't help but smile to herself at being referred to as Lady Carlisle. She would never tire of hearing it.

Mrs. Banks grabbed the edges of her apron and curtsied. "My lady. Everything is just as his lordship directed. A light repast is ready for you in your private sitting room."

Charlotte nodded, but her stomach sank. Was she to eat alone, then? She wanted to voice her question to Edward, but not in front of the servants.

They went inside and Mr. Banks took their gloves, cloaks, and hats. Mrs. Banks was hovering near the stairs, expectantly waiting for Charlotte, it seemed. Charlotte's suspicions were confirmed when Mrs. Banks spoke up.

"I'll show you to your chambers," she said, bobbing another curtsy when Charlotte looked her way.

Edward smiled down at her. "Go with Mrs. Banks. I'm sure you want to freshen up after our drive."

"Will you join me in my sitting room? I'm happy to share a tray with you." Charlotte was trying to put a playful tone to her request, but it sounded more like pleading. She'd hoped to spend at least their first evening as a married couple together.

Thunder rumbled in the distance. "Be sure you build up the fire for the viscountess," Edward instructed before he turned back to her. "I've a few things to attend to, but I'll look in on you before I retire for the evening."

With that, Edward bowed and strode down the hall. Charlotte

watched him go, her good mood wilting as he disappeared into another room. With a bit of self-pity in her heart, she suppressed a sigh and followed Mrs. Banks up the stairs. This was not how she imagined her wedding night.

Mrs. Banks led her to a beautiful room at the top of the stairs and down a short hall. It boasted a spacious sitting room with a warm, crackling fire, two wingback chairs set before it and a low table filled with fruit, meats, and cheeses.

Mrs. Banks paused in the outer room for only a moment before stepping through to the bedchamber. A large canopied bed was in the middle, with doors in the opposite corner that led to a balcony. Needing some air, Charlotte walked over and opened one of them. She stepped to the edge of the balcony and looked out over a small but beautifully arranged flower garden. She inhaled deeply.

"Is there anything else, my lady?" Mrs. Banks appeared at her elbow.

"Yes, I'd like my tray brought out here." Charlotte motioned to the small table with two chairs to her right. "The breeze is picking up, but it's still a beautiful evening."

Mrs. Banks sniffed. "Smells like rain's a-coming. But I'm sure it was the perfect day for a wedding. I'm glad rainy weather didn't interfere with your nuptials."

Mrs. Banks bustled back into the sitting room to retrieve the tray, and her words echoed through Charlotte's mind. The weather hadn't ruined her wedding day at all. It truly had been perfect. Edward had been attentive, and the kiss he'd given her after their vows were spoken had made her want to melt in his arms no matter who was watching. Afterward, he'd held her so close in the carriage. For a few hours it was as if he'd never gone to war and they were living the dream they'd long talked about. But once they'd gotten to Rose Cottage, the walls he'd built between them had reappeared, and he seemed once more like a stranger.

With another sigh, she sat in the chair on the balcony, watching as Mrs. Banks arranged a plate for her on the small table. Yet Charlotte's thoughts were filled with questions, the most important being how could she reach Edward?

"Can I get anything else for you, my lady?" Mrs. Banks asked, her kind eyes watching Charlotte closely.

"No, you've thought of everything." Charlotte pushed a piece of apple to the other side of the cheese. She didn't really have an appetite, but Mrs. Banks had obviously gone to a lot of trouble to provide such a varied meal after her trip. She was a competent housekeeper and good at playing lady's maid for her this evening as well.

"Don't look so troubled," Mrs. Banks said with a motherly smile. "Master Edward is just giving you time to yourself. To get ready." She winked. "I've known him since he was a lad, and I'm so pleased he's finally taken a wife. And don't you worry. I was nervous on my wedding night, but it all worked out. Especially when it's a love match, which anyone can plainly see is what's between you and Master Edward." She fixed a cup of tea and set it next to Charlotte. "Now, if you need any help getting out of your traveling clothes and into your nightdress this evening, you only have to ring for me."

Mrs. Banks patted her on the shoulder as she took her leave. Charlotte didn't know what to say, so she said nothing. Mrs. Banks was right in that it was a love match, but there were definitely some extraordinary circumstances that Charlotte couldn't explain to anyone else. She was still trying to understand them herself. She did know one thing, however. Edward had retreated into himself again, and Charlotte couldn't decide how far to press him. She wanted to have his company this evening, but did he feel the same?

Charlotte ate slowly, listening for Edward's boots on the stairs. Darkness fell quickly and lightning strikes could be seen in the distance. The air grew cold and thunder began to rumble close by, so she went inside and secured the doors. Should she call Mrs. Banks back and get ready for bed? Wander about and find Edward? She decided on the latter.

Opening her bedchamber door, she stepped into the hall and made her way downstairs. All was quiet, the only light coming from under one door in the middle of the hall. Charlotte knocked lightly, but didn't wait for a reply and walked in. "Edward?"

He stood quickly at her entrance, nearly stumbling, but catching himself. "Charlotte. What are you doing here?"

He'd taken off his cravat and waistcoat and rolled his shirt-sleeves to his forearms. His hair was mussed, as if he'd run his hands through it over and over.

She frowned and went to his side. "Edward, what's wrong? Has something happened?"

He moved away from her toward the large window, but seemed to change his mind and spun on his heel to face her again. "It would be best if you went back to your room."

Thunder rumbled again and rain began to patter against the windows behind him. He flinched, as if in pain, and Charlotte closed the distance between them. "Come and sit down with me."

She tugged his arm toward the small sofa in the corner of the room. Edward hesitated, then let her lead him to it. Once they were seated, she took his hand in hers and laced their fingers together. She sat quietly for a moment, listening to the rain. When thunder started to rumble outside, his hand tensed in hers. Was his distress something to do with the storm? As children, they'd often been caught in storms. They had never bothered him before.

"Tell me what's wrong," she said, her voice low.

Edward closed his eyes. "I can't abide storms." His chest rose and fell with rapid breaths. "I'd hoped to spare you seeing your new husband in such a state."

Charlotte drew closer and looked down at his hand in hers. He was trembling. "It is precisely how I should see my new husband. We can face this difficulty together. You only have to trust me as I trust you." She lifted her eyes to his. "I'm not a wilting flower. You can tell me anything."

"This isn't something I want to recall, but I can't get away from the memories. They've followed me home from Spain and plague me mercilessly." He ran his hand through his hair again. "It's . . . The thunder sounds like cannon fire when I hear it. It's like my body is immediately back in Spain." Blowing out a breath, he stared at the blackness beyond the window. "Sometimes the bombardments would last the night, the explosions ripping through the lines, maiming the men I was supposed to protect. There was always a heaviness to the air, just like right before a thunderstorm." Another crack of thunder sounded through the window, and the house seemed to shake with it. Sweat beaded on Edward's brow.

"What can I do?" She wanted with everything she had to comfort him somehow. Leaning in, she pressed close to him.

"I usually drink myself to oblivion," he told her, "but I've decided not to do that anymore. I want to overcome this weakness."

"Then we'll overcome it together, though I don't see it as a weakness. It seems like an unseen wound from your time at war. And nothing to be ashamed of." She met his eyes. Did he believe her?

"Charlotte, I wanted to protect you from knowing what I've become. If you weren't here, I'd probably be cowering under the desk." He blew out a breath. "A fine way to start our marriage, having you see me tremble like a badly made blanc-mange."

Charlotte brushed aside his words. "Remember how we used to play hide-and-seek? And when you found me, you'd hide with me for a moment alone?" She looked down at their intertwined hands. "Perhaps we could both hide under the desk and pretend David is seeking us."

Edward put his arm around her and kissed the top of her head. "You always seemed to hide in the spot where I would first look for you."

Charlotte chuckled, relaxing in his arms. "You didn't seem to mind."

"No, I didn't." Another rumble sounded overhead and Edward tensed.

She kept the conversation going, taking his focus away from the storm. "It was the only time we had away from David's watchful eyes. He had the misguided notion that he had to protect me from you." Charlotte traced her thumb over his knuckles, willing him to stay with her. To remember the good times.

"He had good instincts. Knew me too well." Edward's voice was far away. How could she keep him here with her and not let him fall prey to the difficult memories from his time in Spain?

"I seem to remember how badly I wanted you to kiss me, then." She leaned up and touched his chin, tilting it toward her. Edward's eyes were still watching the window behind her. "Edward," she said softly, touching his cheek. When he met her gaze, she brought her face close to his. "I've missed you so."

His eyes fixed on her, and he caressed her cheek. All the butterflies that had been fluttering in her middle since their wedding vows suddenly came to life again. The rain seemed to be subsiding, but the air was still charged with energy that didn't have anything to do with the storm. Her hand crept up to the nape of his neck. Edward glanced down at her mouth and Charlotte closed her eyes just as his lips met hers.

In the years he'd been gone to war, Charlotte had gone over each kiss they'd ever shared. She'd relived them over and over, keeping those feelings close. But kissing Edward now wasn't anything like she remembered. His lips had started a fire in her blood that was racing through her body, and she couldn't stop it. He cradled her face in his hands, his touch soft and reverent, before putting his arms around her and kissing her deeply. She pressed closer, her fingers running through his hair. She wanted more. Wanted him. But Edward pulled back and leaned his forehead against hers. His breath was coming as fast as hers. "I'm undone."

"Because of me or the storm?" Her voice sounded shaky, but she smiled.

"Both." He put his arm around her shoulder and she settled at his side.

The rain was only a light pitter patter on the window; the storm seemed to be abating. They'd passed their first test as a couple, and it gave Charlotte hope.

Maybe this could be the marriage she'd once dreamed of after all.

CHAPTER 15

*E*dward tucked the lap rug more securely around
Charlotte as the carriage rumbled down the road. They'd
left the cottage early that morning and were nearly to London.
Charlotte had been asleep within the first hour, and Edward had
watched the sun rise with her head resting on his shoulder. It felt
good to have her near. When the thunderstorm had started last
evening, he'd closeted himself in the study, not wanting Charlotte
to see his deep anxiety. He'd vowed not to use alcohol anymore to
dull the fear and pain, but it had taken every ounce of will he had
not to drink the entire bottle of brandy. When Charlotte had come
in, she hadn't been shocked at his disheveled appearance or shaking, but instead had distracted him with her presence.

And her kiss.

He'd always enjoyed stealing a kiss or two from Charlotte, but
last night had been different. He'd never felt anything like that
before---as if her kiss had branded him. Marked him hers.

Edward looked down at her sleeping form. They were still
getting to know one another again, but her familiarity had

comforted him and reminded him of what they'd once shared. Could they truly find their love again?

It wasn't long before the carriage rolled up to Carlisle House and Edward gently shook Charlotte awake. "We're here."

She smiled up at him, her eyes heavy with sleep. "Good morning, husband."

His heart squeezed at hearing her call him husband. He'd never get used to that title. "It's nearly afternoon, my sleeping beauty."

She blushed prettily and sat up. "I'm sorry to have been such a dreadful traveling companion."

"On the contrary, I quite enjoyed the view." He grinned at the deepening of her blush.

The footman opened the door and set down the steps. Edward alighted first, then reached back for Charlotte.

She got out of the carriage and looked up and down the street, relief filling her features. "No one seems to be paying us attention. The last time I was in London . . ."

Edward drew her hand through his arm and led her to the front of the townhouse. "Well, you're returning as a viscountess, so all of that is behind you now." He would make sure she had no reason to fret. He would stand beside her and support her in every way.

Charlotte didn't contradict him though he could feel how rigid the muscles of her arm were as they approached the door. Did she not believe that society would accept her under the protection of his name?

Lambson, the butler opened the door for them, but before they went in, Edward stopped and turned Charlotte toward him. He looked down into her eyes, wishing the happiness he'd seen on her face moments ago were still there.

"I'll do everything in my power to protect you, Charlotte," he said softly.

"I know." She gave him a small smile and they went in the house. The butler took their outside things, and Edward decided to take her to the family sitting room. "Have Cook send up a tray to the blue room," Edward instructed Lambson.

"Very good, my lord," he said before retreating.

Edward escorted Charlotte up the stairs and opened the door. The sitting room was cozy, decorated in different shades of blue. The windows let in a lot of light, which was why it had always been Edward's favorite. Charlotte stayed near his side as he took a seat on the sofa near the hearth.

"What a beautiful room," Charlotte said, as she smoothed the skirts of her deep blue traveling dress and settled next to him. "After our tea, I'll go up and change. Then perhaps we can take a tour of the house?"

Before Edward could reply, the butler entered with a card on a silver salver. He offered it to Edward, who didn't have to look. It was Wolverton's card. How had he known they'd arrived? Did he have someone watching for their arrival? "Send him up, Lambson."

Lambson walked to the door, but Wolverton hadn't waited in the entryway and was instead, standing in the hall just outside the room.

"Come in," Edward said, standing up to greet his guest and letting out a breath. The room lost some of the light and warmth when he saw Wolverton enter and brought him back to reality. Edward wasn't on a wedding trip with Charlotte. He was here to find Marcus. He would do well to remember that.

Wolverton was impeccably dressed in a deep brown coat with tan breeches. His boots were shined to perfection. He looked every inch the marquess, but his lips were pressed together in a slight grimace. He crossed the room to where Edward and Charlotte now stood. "I apologize for intruding, but I didn't want to wait a moment longer."

"Shall we sit?" Edward offered, taking his seat next to Charlotte again. Wolverton took the wingback chair across from them. "Has there been any news?"

Wolverton glanced at Charlotte and then back at Edward, an unspoken question in his gaze. Edward nodded his head slightly. He wanted Charlotte to stay.

"There has been a development," Wolverton said slowly.

That didn't sound like it was a good development. Edward's pulse quickened. "What is it?"

"I talked with my source this morning. He says the French lieutenant was smuggled aboard a ship that landed in Brighton three days ago. He had a wounded man with him and they were headed to London." Wolverton leaned in. "And I received a ransom note this morning."

Edward felt as if he couldn't draw in a breath of air. "What did it say? How much do they want?" he finally managed to get out.

Charlotte stretched her fingers under his grip, and he loosened his hold. He hadn't realized how tightly he'd been holding her hand.

"I'm to bring ten thousand pounds to a gin shop in Seven Dials." Wolverton's mouth drew together in a tight line.

"I'll pay it." Edward ran a hand over his jaw. "I'll sell whatever I have that's not entailed to get the money."

Wolverton held up a hand. "That won't be necessary. I've been putting together a plan while waiting for your arrival. Reasonably, I couldn't bring that kind of money to Seven Dials and not expect to be killed for it." Wolverton plucked at the cuff of his jacket. "I'd like to bluff our little French lieutenant with a forged bank draft and hope he takes the bait. Once we give him the draft, we'll get Marcus somewhere safe."

"When is this meeting to take place?" Charlotte asked. She

discreetly stroked Edward's hand in soothing circles, and he found himself relaxing a little at her touch.

"Tonight." Wolverton looked at Edward. "I was asked to come alone."

"Which no reasonable man would do." Energy flowed through his body, until he thought he might burst from his skin. He stood and began to pace. "Do you think he might bring Marcus to the exchange?" Edward closed his eyes. "I couldn't bring him home from Spain, but I want to bring him home today. No matter what the cost."

"It could be dangerous," Wolverton said, rising and coming to stand next to Edward. "Are you sure?"

Edward met his former commanding officer's gaze. "I've never been more sure of anything in my life."

Wolverton put his hand on Edward's shoulder. "I've got someone working on the forged bank draft. I'd like to scout out the meeting place before we arrive this evening."

Edward glanced at Charlotte. She nodded. "Don't worry about me," she said, folding her hands in her lap. "I'll just get settled here while you're away."

For the briefest moment, Edward wished he could stay with her. Cozying up in the sitting room with Charlotte, some biscuits, and a tea tray, sounded like the perfect afternoon. But Marcus needed him now.

"Hopefully when I return, I'll have Marcus at my side." Edward reached for Charlotte's hand and kissed the back of it before he led the way out of the room. Lambson was gathering his hat and gloves as he made it to the bottom of the stairs with Wolverton on his heels.

"I'm sorry to take you away from home when you've only just arrived," Wolverton said as they put on their hats.

"Charlotte understands." Edward hoped she did, anyway. They

walked out onto the sidewalk, and Wolverton nodded to his driver, who was waiting in front of the townhouse.

As they got into the carriage and sat on either side, Edward leaned back against the squabs. "Why would *you* get the ransom note? That seems strange."

"Whoever this man is, he obviously knows a lot about Marcus's life in the army and that I was his commanding officer," Wolverton said. "I have a title, as well, so they're assuming I can pay, where Marcus's father is a steward and wouldn't have access to such a large sum." He looked gravely at Edward. "I only hope the man got the information in a civilized way and that it wasn't coerced."

"I agree." Edward peered out the window. There was a real possibility that Marcus had endured torture. But he hoped not.

The street vendors called out their wares as they passed. The city was bustling with men and women shopping and conducting business. Life had gone on and Edward had been letting it pass him by. No longer.

Wolverton shifted in his seat and followed Edward's gaze to the street. "You know, you aren't to blame for what happened to Marcus. Guilt can be a slippery thing that pulls you down, but I hope you realize that your actions were honorable." He folded his arms, looking more like the commanding officer Edward remembered. "Marcus is a strong man. His wounds were severe and would have killed an ordinary soldier, but he survived. If he is here in London, we'll find him and get him back."

Edward turned to look at him. "What will happen to his captor?"

"We'll turn him over to the Home Office. I'm sure they would be happy to find out any secrets the lieutenant might have." Wolverton leaned forward, his eyes focused on Edward. "Hopefully Marcus is back with us tonight."

"Thank you for including me in his rescue." Edward gave a

short nod. Bringing Marcus home was all he could think of now. He hadn't been able to save him on the battlefield, but he'd do everything he could to have him back.

The carriage pulled up in front of a nondescript building, and Wolverton got out. "We need to change and check on the forgery before we go into Seven Dials."

Edward frowned. Wolverton talked of forgeries as if they were a normal everyday occurrence. He looked down at his clothes. Wolverton's instructions to change before going to a gin house did make sense. They would stand out in gentlemen's clothing. But what was this building they'd stopped at?

Wolverton led him downstairs to the servants' entrance. They went through an unlocked door and entered a hallway that led to a clean and tidy kitchen.

"Is this one of your bachelor apartments?" Edward asked.

Wolverton looked around the room. "Something like that." He grabbed a bundle from the corner of the room and tossed a second one to Edward. "I took the liberty of guessing that your clothing would be a similar size to mine. You can change in the room behind you."

Edward turned and ducked through the doorway Wolverton had indicated. He stepped into what was possibly a servant's sitting room, but it wasn't at all cozy, the only furniture being a worn sofa. Edward untied the bundle. It held homespun wool trousers and a shirt with mended elbows. He quickly put them on and rejoined Wolverton, who was dressed similarly. "Will the owners of the clothing mind that we've borrowed them?"

"Not at all." Wolverton grinned. "You look quite different."

"As do you, Marquess." Edward bowed, then smiled. This was turning out to be quite the adventure. "Where are the servants?"

"Don't worry about them." Wolverton pushed over a pair of well-used work boots. "We can't appear in our Hessians or they'll give us away, so we'll wear these tonight. But have no doubt, I'll return your belongings to you."

They put the finishing touches on their disguises, and Wolverton picked up a paper from the table that looked like a bank draft. Had his forger been here? What exactly was this place? But Edward didn't ask, and Wolverton didn't elaborate. He merely led them back the way they'd come. The boots pinched Edward's toes a bit as they had to walk a fair ways before they could hail a hack.

"Stay alert and keep your head down," Wolverton warned as they climbed inside.

Wolverton had said the same phrase before every battle. It was just like old times. "Yes, sir," Edward said, feeling the urge to salute. It was good to be in the commander's company and feel like he had a purpose again.

The hack took them to the edge of Seven Dials and the men got out. Wolverton flipped a coin to the jarvey, and they set off. Dusk was just beginning to fall, and shadows hid some of the people loitering in doorways. There was such a sense of despair, it seeped into every corner. Edward pulled his hat lower and kept close to Wolverton.

"There it is." Wolverton stepped around a corner of an abandoned building and looked down the street. Edward cautiously followed behind him. The building didn't have any sign of life at all, except for a cat sniffing for food along a windowsill, yet Edward still felt eyes watching them. Wolverton didn't seem to notice and motioned toward the gin house three doors down.

Light spilled from inside and a few men were milling about out front. Occasionally someone would enter while the loiterers looked on, obvious envy in their faces directed at those going in. Did they not have any money to buy themselves a drink? Is that why they were standing outside?

"Are we going to go in?" Edward whispered. He didn't know why he was whispering. It wasn't as if anyone could hear him.

"Yes. I just want to circle around back and look at the exits first in case we need to leave in a hurry or if our French lieutenant tries to run away." Wolverton walked on, his arms loose at his side and his eyes sweeping the area. No one paid them any attention as they moved to the back of the gin house. There looked to be one exit there that consisted of a thin, wooden door.

"There is a knife hidden on the side of your boot," Wolverton told him without turning around.

Edward leaned down and felt for it. He pulled out the hard metal handle and could see the knife was small, but sharp and lethal. "What do you want me to do?"

"I'll meet with the lieutenant. You stand at the counter and keep watch, but don't be obvious about it. If anything goes wrong, you'll have to help me subdue him. Or, if Marcus is there, you'll take him away as soon as you safely can." Wolverton walked back the way they'd come. The door of the gin house was just to their left and the same men were still standing around the entrance.

Wolverton turned around and touched Edward's arm. "Don't take any unnecessary risks."

Edward inclined his head, though he knew he'd do anything to get Marcus out safely. He would count any such risk as necessary.

"Wait around the corner for a few minutes, then come inside," Wolverton instructed.

Edward did as he was told, waiting until Wolverton had been in the gin house for at least five minutes before he passed the men standing around and walked into the gin house. He was hit with the smell of unwashed bodies and gin. He moved to the long counter and ordered a drink.

Leaning against the stained counter while he waited, Edward scanned the room. Strangely, the room had no chairs, so some patrons were sitting on the floor, others stood in the corners. There were hardly any conversations at all, as everyone seemed focused on the drink in their hands. Wolverton was huddled in a corner with a small man who had a beaked nose, large eyes, and a military bearing. He must be the lieutenant.

The bartender handed them a cloudy glass filled with gin. Wolverton met his gaze briefly, but didn't signal him that anything was wrong. Edward continued to watch, trying to be subtle about his observation, and looking at each patron in case Marcus was nearby. He definitely wasn't in the room.

Wolverton had the bank draft in his hand, but the small man backed up and turned as if to run. Wolverton held his arm. "Not yet," he said, loud enough for Edward to hear.

But the man pulled away and shouldered through the crowd to the front door. Edward stepped in front of him. "I don't think you're finished here."

The small man looked up and fear flashed in his eyes. "Like I told ze other gent, I just want to start a new life. I was helping the English officer to get home, zat's all."

His accent wasn't as thick as Edward had expected, but at the mention of the English officer, Edward grabbed him by his shirt-front. "Where is the English officer?"

The man lifted his chin proudly. "I don't know where he iz. He told me goodbye, just zis morning. He was very angry I asked for money, you see. He didn't want anyone to know he was alive." He looked back at Wolverton who had joined them. "I swear it. I would never hurt Monsieur Harper. He helped me get here to England to start my new life, and I helped him come home so he could die here."

Edward pulled him closer until they were nearly nose to nose. Would he be able to tell if the man was lying? "Is he injured, then?"

The man shrank, his bravado gone. "He has many wounds, yes.

He refuses all ze medical attentions. He only wants to die on English soil."

Edward let him go and the man stumbled back. "And he did not leave his direction? Any hint at where he was going?"

"No." The man straightened his shirt, looking around at the crowd who had given them a wide berth. Some had lifted their eyes from their drinks to see the disturbance, but most kept to themselves. "I'll just be going now." He started to back away, but Edward took hold of his arm once more.

"What's your name?" Edward asked.

"Lieutenant Brunet." The man gave him a slight bow. "I would like to live the rest of my life quietly in Britain. My mother was British, you see, and she always longed to return to her homeland, just like Monsieur Harper. My mother died before she could come, so I am here in her place."

Edward wanted to have a reason not to believe the lieutenant, to have him admit that Marcus was really nearby, but his story rang true. Marcus had apparently disappeared. "If you see or hear from him, please report it to me at Carlisle House," he said, keeping his voice low. "There is a purse with coin in it for you. And thank you. Thank you for bringing him home."

The man nodded and disappeared into the crowd. Edward's shoulders sagged. He was happy that they'd gotten information on Marcus, but he'd hoped for a much better end to this evening.

The crowd began pressing in on them, and Edward felt his panic start to rise. People were all around, in every direction, and the walls were closing in on him. "I need to leave," he said to Wolverton before he started moving toward the door.

Once outside, he took measured breaths to calm his heart.

Wolverton watched him for a moment, but didn't comment. While he waited for Edward to breathe easier, he kept a close eye on the other men near them.

"We need to keep moving," Wolverton finally said, when the crowd swelled to a dozen men or more right outside the gin house.

Edward followed him down an alley. Seven Dials was full of warrens that pickpockets and criminals could hide in, but Wolverton seemed to know where he was going. They did their best to keep to the shadows, meeting few others. Edward wanted to stop and look at every face they did encounter and call out to the ones he could feel watching them from the darkness. Was Marcus close by? But he just kept walking.

Once they gained the street just outside the entrance to the Dials, Wolverton hailed a hack, and they got in. "I'll check with my sources in the morning to see if we can get a lead on Marcus," Wolverton told him.

Edward nodded, but discouragement prevented him from speaking. Lieutenant Brunet had said Marcus didn't want anyone to know he was alive. If that was the case, their chances of finding him were slim.

But he wouldn't give up.

Edward had gone over and over that last day at the church in Spain, feeling the weight of guilt that he'd left Marcus behind. He never wanted to feel that way again.

He would search every corner of London if he had to. He was going to find Marcus, even if it took the rest of his life. He wouldn't walk away. Not this time.

CHAPTER 16

*A*fter Edward and Wolverton left, Charlotte spent the day touring the house with the housekeeper and meeting the rest of the staff. She'd overseen her trunks being unpacked and had even had a lie-down. But now it was dark and Edward still wasn't home. Was he still with Lord Wolverton? Had he gone to a gentlemen's club? There were so many things she didn't know about her new husband's habits.

She sat in an overstuffed chair in the library and debated sending her mother a note that she'd arrived safely. But getting out her writing materials didn't suit her mood. Perhaps she could find a book to distract herself? Before she could decide on an activity, there was a knock at the door. "Enter."

The butler peered in at her. "Would you like a tray brought to your chambers, my lady? Or would you like to have dinner served in the dining room?"

The thought of eating alone in a large room didn't appeal at all. "I'd like a tray brought in here." The butler nodded and shut the door behind him.

Charlotte looked around the library. The large hearth had several chairs strategically placed around it, and the shelves were full of every book imaginable. There were several windows to let in light, and the gold window coverings perfectly complemented the deep burgundy of the upholstery. It was comfortable and looked well-used. Did Edward while away his time in here?

The door opened again and Charlotte didn't look up at the servant bringing in the tray. "Just put it on the low table," she instructed. "And please inform me when the viscount arrives home."

The maid set the tray down, then straightened to address her. "The viscount arrived home an hour ago, my lady. He went straight to his bedchambers." She bobbed a curtsy and withdrew.

Charlotte frowned. Why wouldn't Edward seek her out? And how had she missed his arrival? Rising, she decided to go to him. She wanted to hear how the meeting had gone with the Frenchman. Since Marcus hadn't come home with him, it plainly hadn't gone as Edward had hoped. Maybe that's why he'd wanted to be alone. Well, she could offer him comfort.

Picking up her skirts, she walked upstairs to Edward's bedchamber. When she reached his door, she knocked softly, but didn't hear any response from inside. Did she dare enter? Deciding she did, Charlotte turned the door handle. His room was dark, with only the fire burning low in the fireplace to light her way forward.

Edward was lying on the bed fast asleep, his breathing slow and even. He was still fully clothed, though he was now wearing a stained shirt and wool trousers that didn't belong to him. They were obviously work clothes, but where had he gotten them? What had happened?

She tiptoed closer and stood next to the bed. He looked so boyish when he was relaxed in slumber. It was endearing to see him thus. She reached out to gently brush his hair back from his forehead, but his hand snaked out and grabbed her wrist, quickly flipping her onto the bed before she could let out a squeak of surprise.

He caged her underneath him, his hand wrapped around her throat. "What are you doing in my tent? Trying to steal something?" he ground out.

Tent? What did he mean? Charlotte looked up at him. His eyes were open, but wide and unseeing. "Edward," she gasped. "It's Charlotte. We're at home, in London." She pulled at the hand on her throat. "Please."

Edward blinked and slowly came to awareness. When he saw her face, he paled and pulled away, stricken. "Charlotte?" He knelt on the bed, his hand covering his mouth. He seemed to be gasping for air. "Oh, Charlotte. Please tell me I didn't injure you."

His pained expression pulled on her heartstrings. She sat up carefully, her hand at her throat. "No, of course you didn't."

His eyes narrowed in disbelief and he moved closer to gently pull the hand away that covered her neck. "That's my handprint on your skin." Revulsion filled his voice. "I could have killed you." He nearly leaped from the bed and stepped back as though he didn't trust himself to be close to her.

She reached for him, hoping he'd take her hand. He didn't and she let it fall. "Edward, I'm fine. Please don't worry. I surprised you while you were sleeping, that's all. Look at me. I'm quite all right."

He didn't meet her pleading gaze, just shook his head from side to side. Rubbing a hand against the front of his work shirt, right over his heart, he finally glanced up. "I should have realized that you're not safe with me." He backed away until he was at the door. "I never thought I would . . . I can't be here." And he opened the door, slamming it shut behind him.

Charlotte gaped at the place where he'd stood, but she quickly got off the bed and opened the door to follow him, determination in her steps. They needed to discuss this right now. She feared if they didn't, it would always be between them. She didn't want him to ever be afraid he would harm her.

But he wasn't in the hallway, the dining room, or the parlor. The butler nodded as she approached the entryway. She hated to ask the staff where her husband was, but she had no choice. "Have you seen the viscount?"

"He's gone out, my lady." The butler didn't give her any indication that it was out of the ordinary for a newly married bride to not know the location of her groom.

"Did he say where?"

"No, my lady." His eyes were kind. "Is there anything else I can help you with?"

"No." She turned to go back to the library, then thought the better of it. "Will you send my maid to my room? I've decided to retire early."

"Yes, my lady."

Charlotte climbed the stairs, weary in mind and spirit. The incident in the bedchamber had shown her exactly what Edward was struggling with, and he'd probably been fearful from the beginning that he would harm her somehow. All she wanted to do now was reassure him that he would never hurt her purposely. She'd been startled, that's all, and the moment Edward recognized her, he'd let her go. Charlotte wasn't frightened of him. They could get through this. If only she knew where he'd gone.

She opened the door to her chambers and bypassed the sitting room, going straight to her dressing table. She sat at the stool and looked into the mirror, letting her elbow rest on the table, her head in her palm. Outwardly, she looked serene and in control. Inwardly, her insides were churning with emotion. How could she show Edward that she wasn't as fragile as he thought? How she wished she'd moved to his side the moment he'd backed away. Perhaps she could have made him see that she wasn't hurt. Tilting her head, she looked at her neck, running her fingers over the skin. The handprint was nearly faded and there wouldn't be any bruising. It was all just a misunderstanding. She let out a deep sigh.

Her new maid, Millie, entered the room and stood behind her. When Charlotte didn't move or give her any instructions, she furrowed her brow. "Shall I brush out your hair, my lady? Or would you prefer to put on your nightdress first?"

Charlotte raised her head. "I've changed my mind, Millie. I'm going to wait for my husband in the study." They needed a second chance to talk, and when they spoke again, she was determined to work toward an understanding between them.

Millie looked confused but bobbed a curtsy. "Yes, my lady."

"Please light a fire in the room. I'll be there shortly." When Edward came back, he'd likely go straight to his study for a retreat. If he didn't, she'd be able to hear his footsteps going up to his chambers. It was the perfect position.

Millie left to do her bidding, and Charlotte walked slowly back down the stairs. The portraits of the former viscounts seemed to follow her footsteps. *Were theirs happy marriages?* she wondered as she looked into their faces. None of them had probably dealt with the circumstances between her and Edward, though. But there had to be a way forward and Charlotte was going to find it.

She walked into the study and sat in the chair behind the desk. The well-worn leather creaked as she settled into it. Running her hands over the mahogany finish, she imagined Edward sitting there, going over his ledgers. Would he be surprised to find her in here when he returned?

But as the night wore on and Edward didn't come home, Charlotte began to despair. Where could he be? She thought of retiring to her bed, then stiffened her spine. She would wait.

When the clock chimed two in the morning, Charlotte was awakened by the door opening. She lifted her head and rubbed the back of her neck. She'd fallen asleep at the desk.

Edward stumbled into the room and stopped at the sight of her. "Charlie!" He nearly fell over the chair in front of the desk, but caught himself just in time. "What are you doing here?"

Charlotte stood and came around the desk where the stench of liquor hit her full force. Edward was foxed. "I was waiting for you," she said quietly.

Edward shook his head. "You sh-should be schleeping." He was slurring his words and looked up at her owlishly. "You don't want to be around me. I'm a danger to you."

Charlotte tentatively reached out and laid her hand on his sleeve. "You would never hurt me Edward. Never."

He coughed and swallowed. "I already did. I knew I would. That's why I wanted to break the betrothal. So you wouldn't s-schee what I've become," he informed her, as he brushed by her and opened the liquor cabinet behind the desk. "But I couldn't stay away and now look what I've done." He poured two fingers of whiskey into a tumbler and held it aloft as if making a toast. "We haven't even been married a week and I've already caused you injury."

Charlotte took the glass from him. "I think you've had enough."

He plucked it right back from her. "I think I'm just getting started. A good whiskey always makes me feel better."

Charlotte remembered him saying during the storm that he was trying not to use liquor to fight against his demons anymore. Tonight must have been too much if he'd sought comfort from a bottle. Her heart ached for him. "Let me help you, Edward. Please."

He ran a hand over his face at her plea. "It's best that you s-schtay far away from me, Charlotte. I-I'm not fit to be your husband. You're better off without me."

She went to his side, wishing she dared put her arms around him. "Why don't we go down to the kitchen and get some coffee for you."

"No, I don't want coffee. I don't want anything. I don't want to feel anything." He staggered away and sat down on the sofa, as if he couldn't stand any longer, then laid his head back on the cushion. "I'm sorry, Charlotte."

The last came out as a near whisper and Charlotte sat next to him. Pushing his hair back from his face, she had so many emotions running through her. The alcohol had loosened his tongue enough to share the root of what was bothering him and she knew they could get past it. If only he would let her help.

"I'll go make a pot of coffee for you and be right back," she said softly.

"Don't go." He reached an arm around her shoulders and pulled her close. "My Charlotte."

It didn't matter that he was foxed; his words warmed her heart. He wanted her with him and had called her his Charlotte. She let herself be held and rested her head on his chest. "Edward, you know I'll stay with you, but we must have a long talk tomorrow. If we're to go on with this marriage, we must discuss our expectations." She waited for a response, but got a snore instead. She looked up at his face. He was sleeping.

With a deep sigh, she relaxed in his embrace. They'd had a difficult start to their marriage, but not in the ways she'd expected. Charlotte had thought they would have trouble finding Marcus and getting to know one another again. She couldn't have imagined the trials Edward had been facing alone and she'd likely never have known if she hadn't been his wife.

Charlotte shifted slightly and his arm tightened around her, as if making sure she stayed by his side. No matter what he said, she wasn't better off without him. He was her husband now, and they needed to stay together more than ever.

Tomorrow she would convince him to truly let her in and accept her help. But tonight, she'd enjoy being in her husband's arms for just a while longer.

CHAPTER 17

*E*dward opened one eye and groaned. His mouth was as dry as cotton, but at least he wasn't on the floor. The soft cushion underneath him and the painted cherubs frolicking on the ceiling were the clues he needed to discern that he lay on the settee in his study. Bits and pieces of last night came back to him---he'd pinned Charlotte to the bed, his hand around her throat. Then he'd gone to his club where he'd sat alone, drinking until the numbness claimed him. But Charlotte had waited up for him. Here. In the study.

He turned his head slowly. She wasn't in the room now. His fists clenched, and shame flowed through him. Had she left him and gone back to Winslow Hall? He wouldn't have blamed her.

The door opened, and Charlotte came in with a tray. "You're awake," she noted, as she arranged the tray on his desk. "Good. I've brought you a posset, one that David has used many times."

Edward sat up, resisting the urge to lie down again, to close his eyes against the light and the censure he was sure to find in Charlotte's eyes.

"Thank you," he murmured, keeping his gaze on the floor.

Charlotte came and sat next to him, holding out a steaming mug of something that had the faint scent of mint. "David always has a sore head after a night of too much frivolity. This is really the best medicine. I made it myself since I knew you'd be feeling poorly this morning."

She'd made him the posset herself? He couldn't refuse. Taking the cup from her, he was grateful the drink smelled so much better than the one Cook usually made up for him. "You didn't need to trouble yourself."

Charlotte was silent, and he finally gathered his courage to look her in the eye. He didn't see censure there, only concern, and relief filled him. Maybe he hadn't ruined everything between them.

"Of course I would go to the trouble," she finally said. She had changed out of the gown she'd been wearing last night and looked beautiful in a light pink day dress. The color contrasted with her dark hair and made her look quite young and innocent. Quite the opposite of what Edward was feeling this morning---old, sinful, and weary.

She folded her hands in her lap. "Would you like to talk about what happened?"

No, he really wouldn't, but knew he must. "I hurt you Charlotte." He bent to see her neck, grateful there didn't appear to be any sign of injury. "Sometimes I have night terrors when I sleep and I'm back on the battlefield or just trying to survive." He heaved a sigh. "If you'd like to annul the marriage rather than worry for your own safety, I understand."

"Nonsense. Edward, I know you are fighting a great battle, but I wish you'd let me fight beside you." She inched closer until her leg touched his and then she reached out to grasp his arm. "I'm not hurt and I'm not as fragile as I look."

No, she wasn't. He put his hand over her much smaller one that was resting on his forearm. "I know that. It's quite difficult for me to fear what I might do to you when I'm sleeping. I couldn't bear it if I seriously hurt you."

"You wouldn't. You didn't. And I'm not worried at all. We're going to get through this together," she murmured. "Now tell me what happened with the Frenchman. Did he come to the meeting?"

Edward shifted so he could face her. "Yes, but Marcus wasn't with him. Apparently, Marcus became angry that the French lieutenant had alerted us to the fact that he was alive and left without so much as a by-your-leave. So, we have no clues as to where Marcus could have gone."

"What a disappointment," Charlotte said with a frown. "Do you have any idea of where to begin looking?"

Edward wished he did. Before he could say so, a commotion rose in the hallway.

Their butler, Lambson, arrived at the door, out of breath. "The Marquess of Wolverton," he managed to get out before Wolverton appeared in the doorway.

"No need to announce me, my good man." Wolverton walked into the room, but pivoted on his heel to say, "The viscount is expecting me."

"That will be all, Lambson," Edward said. The butler looked miffed at the breach of protocol, but he shut the door with a nod. Edward would have to smooth any ruffled feathers later. Once the door had closed, Edward faced Wolverton. "I wasn't expecting you until later this morning."

"It's nearly noon." Wolverton looked more closely at Edward. "Difficult night?"

"You might say that," Edward said with a grimace. It galled him that Lord Wolverton was seeing him thus. As the commanding officer of Edward's regiment, Wolverton had laid down rules for the men that included no alcohol while they were on campaign. It dulled their senses and weakened the skills they'd learned in training, he'd said. But the alcohol had been the only thing that let him forget the war and his failings.

Edward finished the posset and handed the cup back to Charlotte. "Any news?"

"No." The marquess glanced at Charlotte and she motioned him to the overstuffed chair opposite the settee. He settled in and continued. "Not more than we knew from last night. But my Veterans Club offers a free hot meal once a day, and I suspect that if Marcus is in London, he'll turn up there."

Edward's heart began to pound. Could Marcus find his way to a Veterans Club? "Will we go there to wait for him, then?"

"No. I thought we'd go there to help serve the food. But in your condition . . ." Wolverton's voice trailed off as he shook his head. "That might not be wise."

"I'm fine." Edward straightened. "You cannot leave me out if you think Marcus may turn up."

"I don't want to." Wolverton's brow furrowed and he exhaled. "Edward, this may be extremely presumptuous of me, but may I share a confidence with you?"

"Yes, of course." Edward glanced at Charlotte, and she reached for his hand.

Wolverton shifted in his chair, as if uncomfortable with what he was about to impart to them. He looked at both Charlotte and Edward before he spoke. "When I first returned from Spain, my father was ill, my brother had died, and I was expected to step into my new role of Marquess. I felt overwhelmed and inadequate, so I closeted myself in my father's study, drank all the liquor in the house, and sent for more."

Edward was stunned. Wolverton had always seemed so unruffled. Even through the worst of the battles, Wolverton had been calm and steady, someone who never seemed to need help.

Wolverton took a deep breath. "One morning I woke up, much like you did today I'll wager, and realized I was more than the drink. I was stronger than that. I'd fought for my country, survived, and my family needed me. I had my servants pour out every bit of liquor in my home and I haven't touched any since. When I feel the urge come upon me, I go to the Veterans Club to talk to the men there who have bigger struggles than mine. Or I confide in my wife." Wolverton turned to Charlotte and gave her a small smile. "I wanted to tell you, Lady Carlisle, that my wife, Alice, would like to call on you this afternoon, if that is agreeable. She can hardly wait to meet you."

Charlotte smiled politely. "That would be wonderful. I don't have many connections in Town, and I'd be happy to make her acquaintance."

Edward let Wolverton's words sink into his whiskey-soaked brain. He watched Charlotte's countenance as she spoke to Wolverton. She was genuinely happy at the thought of meeting Alice and didn't sound like she would be packing to leave him and return to Winslow Hall. He wanted to be the one to shelter and protect her, but he couldn't do that if he was foxed. He made up his mind in that moment that he wouldn't touch another drop of alcohol. He owed it to Charlotte. And to himself.

"Thank you for your confidence, Wolverton. I believe that might be the path I should take as well." Edward turned to Charlotte and let his thumb caress the inside of her wrist. "My family needs me, too."

Charlotte's eyes shone with tears, but she was smiling at him. "I'll be here to help you with whatever you need."

"Thank you." He raised her hand to his lips and pressed a brief kiss to her knuckles.

"Lord Wolverton, would it be permissible for me to come along and help serve the meal to the veterans?" Charlotte sniffed delicately, the result of holding back her tears, no doubt, and turned to Wolverton.

"Please, will you not call me Christian?" He inclined his head. "And may I have permission to call you Charlotte?"

"Of course." She ran a hand over her skirts. "So, may I assist you in serving the meal?"

"Yes. I know Alice also enjoys assisting. Perhaps Edward and I could take a tour of the club, and then you and Alice can join us to serve the meal?" Christian settled back into his seat. "And I apologize for spiriting your husband away again so soon, but once this inquiry is over, perhaps you can take a proper wedding trip."

Edward nodded. "Yes, we're planning on that." His chest squeezed at the thought of having Charlotte all to himself on a wedding trip. They'd often talked of it before he'd left for war, and it was one hope that he'd cherished through the long marches. Could he risk being with her in the dark of night? Would his night terrors always be a concern? Perhaps it was as Charlotte said, this was something they needed to decide together. He was willing to try. Charlotte deserved everything he could give her as his wife.

He could trust her. He knew he could.

Charlotte was laughing over something Wolverton had said, but Edward hadn't heard their comments. The throbbing in his head was getting better, however. The posset must have worked, for which he was grateful. He needed to be sober if he was to participate in possibly finding Marcus today.

Christian stood and Charlotte stood with him. Edward gained his feet as well, a bit unsteady, but not staggering, which was a good sign.

"Thank you again for being so understanding," Christian said as he took his leave of Charlotte.

"Take good care of him," Charlotte said softly.

Christian nodded before turning to Edward. "I'm sure you'll want to freshen up a bit before we go to the Veterans Club," Christian said, as he started toward the door. "I'll wait for you in the carriage." And then he left, giving them a bit of privacy to say their goodbyes.

As soon as the door closed, Edward faced Charlotte. "I'm sorry," he said, hoping she could hear the sincerity in his voice. "For last night and for this morning."

"We'll talk more about it tomorrow, when all of this is behind us." Charlotte patted his lapel, smoothing her palm over it. "But please be careful today." She kissed him on the cheek, and he slipped his arms around her waist, liking the feel of her in his arms.

"I will." He raised one hand, wishing he dared to kiss her. Would she accept his attentions after he'd frightened her during his night terror? Perhaps that would be their first topic of discussion. He wanted to lay everything at her feet and ask her to help him decide how best to handle his night terrors and their consequences. Then, he would kiss his wife senseless. Even the thought of kissing Charlotte and eventually having a proper wedding night with her made his heart pound a little faster.

As if she could read his thoughts, Charlotte smiled and squeezed his hand. He left her in the study and went upstairs, calling for Gibbs. His valet was used to dressing him quickly. Hopefully he could perform that duty in double-time today.

As he walked to his chamber, he rolled his shoulders. The burden he'd been carrying for so long seemed to have vanished. Though he hadn't wanted Charlotte to suffer because of him, she'd been marvelously understanding and somehow relieved him of a bit of the weight he carried. He hadn't expected that.

Once Edward was presentable, he went downstairs and

claimed his greatcoat. Stepping outside, he saw Christian's carriage waiting out front. The pain in Edward's head was manageable now, which he was grateful for as he moved toward the carriage. Opening the door, he climbed inside. "Sorry to keep you waiting," he said as he settled in the seat across from Christian.

"Not at all. You look much better." Christian leaned forward to pull back the curtains a bit. "And I'm pleased to show you my Veterans Club. It's not far from here, actually."

Edward felt a little spark of hope that Marcus might be there today. "It's a wonderful idea. I'm sure the men greatly appreciate it."

Christian nodded. "Most do. I just saw soldiers suffering when they tried to return to the life they'd had before the war. Like you, it was a hard road for them and I wanted to do something to make it easier. I like to think the club helps."

The carriage stopped, and Christian got out first. When Edward exited, he looked up at the building in front of him. It was larger than he expected, on the edge of a respectable neighborhood. This was the club?

"Follow me," Christian said, as he climbed the steps. Edward did as he was bid and a butler answered the door.

"Good to see you, Reams," Christian greeted the man, who looked nothing like a butler. He had to be a good head taller than anyone of Edward's acquaintance, and a large scar ran from his eyebrow to his chin, barely missing his eye. It gave him a sinister look, but the man gave Christian a lop-sided smile.

"I'm going to give the viscount a tour. If anyone has need of me, we'll start in the billiards room."

"Very good, sir." Reams opened the door wider and let them through. Edward had to force himself not to stare at the large butler and kept his eyes on the staircase in front of them.

Once they'd gained the upper floor, Edward saw two big rooms on either end of the hallway and four smaller rooms between. Several men were talking in the corridor. They didn't look like anyone from any of his gentleman's clubs. They wore rough clothing. One man was missing an arm, his empty sleeve pinned to his shoulder. But they were smiling and laughing. There wasn't an air of sadness or bitterness to be found.

As they entered the long room to the left, Edward noted two billiards tables at one end and pugilistic equipment on the other. Men crowded around both the billiards being played, and a small square cordoned off that held two men involved in a boxing match. Leather bags hung from the rafters where other men were pummeling them. Spectators were engrossed in the games in front of them and didn't notice Edward and Christian's arrival.

"This club is exclusively for men who have served in the King's army," Christian said as he looked around the room. "My main purpose in creating it was to be able to extend the brotherhood that we found on the battlefield, and use it to confront the problems we all have now that we're home." He turned to Edward. "And as I mentioned earlier, I'd like to help you battle your demons. I've been where you are, and could have used a brother in the fight."

Deep shame filled Edward's heart. He was a man who should be able to take care of himself. But before he could decline, Christian put his hand on Edward's shoulder. "Even now I have nightmares---hearing the shrieks of the dying horses on the field and the groans of the near-dead men beside them. Most men coming home from the war have night terrors, sensitivity to loud sounds, and other trials to varying degrees. But we can all help one another. Feel that brotherhood and support right here." He gestured around the room.

Maybe that brotherhood was just what he needed. Edward looked into his former commander's eyes, wanting to believe in his words.

"You were one of my best men, Edward. You had the strength of heart that we needed in the fight against Napoleon, and you still have it---strength that your brothers-in-arms need from you now, here in England." Christian pinned him with his gaze. "And you can also lean on us." Then he slapped Edward on the back. "Enough. Let me show you the rest of the club."

"Thank you, sir." He stood tall and swallowed, hoping to live up to Christian's high opinion.

They walked down the hall, and Edward looked in the door-ways of the smaller rooms that included a reading library and several small salons. The other large area at the opposite end was a long dining room.

"I employ a full kitchen staff for meals," Christian said, the pride in what the club offered obvious in his voice. "All footmen are former military men, and the maids and cooks are women who have lost husbands in the war and need to support their families." They stopped at the dining table nearest the door. "What do you think?"

"You've done a fine thing here, and I'd be honored to be a part of it." Edward looked around him. The men here had experienced what he had. Perhaps he could lean on them as Christian had said. And he wanted to be the kind of man they could lean on as well.

Something was changing in him today. And he liked it. Now all he had to do was find Marcus and help put away some of the dark feelings left over from the war.

It was the only way forward.

CHAPTER 18

Charlotte sat nervously in the drawing room and brushed her palms over her best day dress. The blues of the carpet and wall hangings were meant to be calming, she was sure, but Charlotte was about to receive the Marchioness of Wolverton. What if the marchioness hadn't learned of the scandal that had surrounded the Pembroke name and left immediately when she did? David had mentioned he'd once sought the lady's favor, but he hadn't said much more. Did the marchioness hold any ill will against Charlotte's family?

The door opened, and Lambson announced Lady Wolverton. Charlotte rose as she entered, giving her best curtsy. "Welcome, my lady."

Lady Wolverton was dressed in a simply cut lavender gown that flattered her figure. The fabric and design was quite obviously the first stare of fashion, yet surprisingly understated, and the color complemented the lady's fair complexion.

Charlotte cleared her throat as the marchioness walked to her side, surprised to see a genuine smile and outstretched arms. "Oh, I hope you'll call me Alice," she said with a tilt of her head. "I want us to be fast friends."

Warmth gathered in Charlotte's chest at the sincerity in the other woman's face, and she straightened. When she'd been out in society, she hadn't met many ladies who spoke of friendship. "I would like that as well. Call me Charlotte."

Alice sat down on the damask sofa just to the side of the fireplace and pulled Charlotte with her like they were old friends who'd been apart for a long while. "Christian told me you are recently married and that he's dragged your husband away on business, so I am here to keep you company. I do apologize, but I hope you know that Christian wouldn't infringe upon your privacy at such a time unless it was very important."

"Of course." A maid appeared in the doorway carrying a tea tray bearing their best tea service. The silver had also been shined to perfection, for which Charlotte was grateful. After all, they were receiving a marchioness.

Charlotte directed the maid to place it on the mahogany table in front of her. There was a selection of biscuits and fairy cakes that looked absolutely divine. She would have to compliment Cook later. "How do you like your tea?" she asked Alice.

"Two sugars and a dash of cream, please."

Charlotte gathered a small plate of biscuits and cakes, then poured Alice's tea. "How long have you been in London?" she asked, trying to think of something to talk about besides the weather. Truthfully, she was still quite shocked at how amiable Alice was. Did she truly not know society's opinion of Charlotte? The taint on the Pembroke name?

"Not long." Alice took a sip of her tea, inhaling the aroma as she did so. "There's nothing as comforting as a good cup of tea, don't you agree?" She glanced at Charlotte, her eyes open and friendly.

"Did you know I'm recently wed myself? We've been in the country since our marriage."

"Yes, I had heard that." But only from her disappointed brother's perspective, which wouldn't be something to speak of in Alice's company. "May I offer my congratulations?"

Alice set her cup down in the saucer. "Thank you. I must say, your brother was most gracious when I turned down his suit." She raised her eyebrows and waved a hand in Charlotte's direction. "I hope that's not at all awkward for you. I told David that very day that I would like to remain friends. I want to extend that offer of friendship to you. I know a little of what your family has endured since David was wrongfully accused. I firmly believe in his innocence and that society has treated you abominably."

The coil of uncertainty Charlotte had been feeling since she learned of Alice's visit eased. She was a remarkable woman. No wonder David had been taken with her. "Thank you. It has been rather difficult."

She took a fairy cake from her plate and bit into it. Charlotte was starting to feel as if she'd known Alice for ages, rather than just a quarter of an hour. She had a way of making her feel at ease.

"Well, I hope you won't be hiding from those old society tabbies," Alice went on. "You're a respectably married woman, and there isn't a good reason for you to avoid being at society events. Perhaps we can even go together when you feel ready." Alice took a bite of a biscuit, her gaze on Charlotte. "We could have great fun."

The other woman's eyes were twinkling with mischief, and Charlotte let herself be caught up in the moment. Perhaps it would be diverting to go to a ball or musicale and show them all she wasn't afraid of their petty gossip. "I would enjoy that." She hadn't thought she'd ever look forward to attending an event in London again. This time, however, she'd be on Edward's arm, with Alice as her friend. Their company would make anything bearable.

"Christian came to collect Edward and mentioned that they would be serving a meal to the veterans at the club. I offered our help in serving the hot meal that will be provided, and your husband agreed." Charlotte flushed. Was that a breach of protocol to volunteer for a marchioness? But Christian hadn't seemed to think it was an untoward suggestion.

"Yes, Christian sent round a note that I'm to escort you to the club." Alice leaned forward in her seat until she was nearly on the edge, as though she was about to impart a great secret. "I quite enjoy being around the old soldiers. They always have a good story to tell. I hope you'll be charmed by them as well."

"Shall I call for our carriage to be brought around?" Charlotte's mouth curved in a smile. Alice's sincerity was refreshing.

"It's not far. Shall we walk? The weather is fine today." Alice rose and Charlotte stood with her.

"That would be lovely." Charlotte couldn't remember the last time she'd strolled down a London street with a friend. This would be a treat.

The two women moved to the entryway where Lambson retrieved their cloaks and bonnets. "Do you spend a lot of time at the club?" Charlotte asked. It was strange to think of a woman in a gentleman's club.

"As much as I can. I have other duties that I must tend to, of course, but I do enjoy an afternoon there whenever I can get away." Alice tied her bonnet under her chin. "It's quite unlike anything you've ever attended. You'll see."

Once they were ready and a footman had been called, they walked out into the weak sunshine. The air was turning colder by the day, and winter wasn't far off. Charlotte pulled her cloak closer around her.

They hadn't walked far when two other ladies approached from the opposite direction. Their lavish hats that featured enough feathers and plumes to stuff a pillow, gave away their identity. Charlotte groaned inwardly. Lady Sarah and Lady Harriet. The last time she'd seen them was during the height of her troubles last Season. They had whispered just loud enough for her to hear the name they had given her: Lady Charlotte of DeadBroke, to remind her that her brother, the Earl of Pembroke, was suspected of murder and their estate was near ruin.

They had tittered behind their fans as if it was a great jest, and appeared to be the leaders in the gossip about her continuing throughout the *ton*. Charlotte had found it too much to bear and had begged David to take her home to Winslow Hall. Though, once home, she'd had to deal with Mrs. Lindstrom from the village, who turned out to be just like the "ladies" of London. Catty behavior could be found in all classes, Charlotte supposed.

She hoped they would only greet each other and keep walking, but Lady Sarah blocked their path, turning just enough so that her back was partially to Charlotte.

"Lady Wolverton, how wonderful to see you in Town. It has been an age!" Lady Sarah gave Alice a deep curtsy and smiled up at her when she rose, completely ignoring Charlotte's presence. Her insult didn't hurt, however. Charlotte could clearly see Lady Sarah's eyes were calculated as she watched Alice, wanting the connection with a marchioness, not friendship. How had Charlotte ever sought to win Lady Sarah's approval or given her opinions any weight? The woman's shallowness was quite clear.

Alice's mouth tightened, though she acknowledged Sarah by inclining her head slightly. "Yes, well, good afternoon."

Charlotte let out a small sigh of relief. Alice didn't seem to want to converse. Perhaps that was the end of it. They started to move away but had hardly gone two steps when Lady Sarah spoke again.

"Lady Charlotte, I admit, I'm surprised to see you in Town as well." Her honeyed tone couldn't hide the spite behind the words. "I was sure you would be staying in the country for quite some time after the . . . well, I don't want to be indelicate, but the *incident* with your brother, Lord De . . . excuse me, Lord Pembroke."

Anger began to swirl through Charlotte at another intended slight, replacing the anxiety that had gripped her. She debated just walking on, but instead, lifted her chin, straightened her spine, and turned slowly to face Lady Sarah. "In case you hadn't heard, my brother was proved innocent of any wrongdoing." Putting a hand to her middle to calm herself and stave off casting up her accounts, she took a deep breath. If Edward could face his fears, she would confront hers as well. "And I am in Town because I recently married and my husband, the Viscount Carlisle, has some business here."

"You finally brought him up to scratch then?" Lady Harriet asked with a snicker. "Haven't you been betrothed for absolutely years and years?"

Lady Sarah lifted her eyebrows. "That *is* a surprise. I had heard Viscount Carlisle wanted to call off the betrothal and thought it might be because of what happened with . . . I can barely speak of it." She turned to Alice. "Well, I'm sure you heard of the taint on the Pembroke name, my lady."

Alice opened her mouth to say something, but Charlotte put a hand on her arm and spoke first. "My husband is a war hero who was away fighting for his country, and as I said, my brother was proved innocent." She took a step closer to Sarah and was gratified to see her eyes widen as she hastily moved back. "And just to be clear, I am the daughter and sister of an earl, not to mention the wife of a viscount. But none of those titles matter because I have love in my life. People who genuinely care for me. True friendship that I can count on. I know you cannot say the same and I daresay there will come a time when you will find yourself quite alone with no one to call on to relieve your loneliness. And it will be your own fault." Charlotte's breaths were coming fast and her heart was pounding, but the look on Sarah's face was priceless.

Alice linked her arm with Charlotte's. "I am lucky to be one of Lady Charlotte's dear friends. Now we really must be on our way."

Neither Charlotte nor Alice offered a proper goodbye, merely turned on their heels and walked away. Charlotte was shocked she'd actually said those things out loud. For so many nights she'd imagined giving Sarah and Harriet that kind of setdown, but hadn't thought she'd ever have the courage to do it. But she had!

"You were magnificent, Charlotte." Alice grinned and squeezed her arm. "I couldn't have said it better. Did you see Sarah's face? She looked like a fish out of water, opening and closing her mouth like that."

Charlotte couldn't help laughing at the image. "She did, didn't she? It felt good to confront them and show that I'm not hiding from their insulting behavior ever again."

"I hope you know you always have an ally in me." Alice tilted her head toward Charlotte's. "And besides, we have much better things to do with our day. We'll not allow anything to ruin it."

Charlotte agreed. It was wonderful to have a friend by her side. "Yes. I'm anxious to see this club and meet the veterans you speak so highly of."

Alice stopped in front of a square building on the right and pushed through a small gate. Once she climbed the front steps, she turned to Charlotte. "Here we are!"

A large man with a scarred face opened the door for them. It was a beastly scar. *He was lucky he hadn't lost an eye*, Charlotte thought.

"Good afternoon, Lady Alice," he said with a bright smile, the scar turning one of his lips downward. He smoothed his coat and bowed to the ladies.

"Good afternoon, Reams," Alice said, dipping her chin in acknowledgment. "I've brought my friend, Lady Charlotte with me today."

"Very good, my lady." He straightened and stood at attention, as if he was still in the military and they were his commanders. "The men will be happy to see a pretty lady at their meal today."

Alice laughed and her eyes sparkled. "You are a charmer. Tell me, how is your sister? Has she written to you recently?"

"She has. Delilah arrived in Surrey and wrote to say that the housekeeper is very kind. Put her to work as an upstairs maid." Reams fairly beamed. "Thank you for recommending her for the position."

Alice didn't hesitate to raise a hand as if to humbly wave away his thanks. "It was no trouble at all. Please keep me informed on her situation. Delilah is such a lovely girl."

"Thank you, my lady." Reams bowed, politely, his high regard for Alice written on his face. "The captain is upstairs."

Alice turned to Charlotte as they walked toward the staircase. "Reams was a soldier in Christian's command. He was horribly wounded after being in Spain for only a month. When Reams arrived home to convalesce, he found his parents had both died of a fever and his sister Delilah was trying to take care of all six of the other children on her own. As soon as Christian heard of the situation, we did what we could to find paid positions for the oldest of them. Reams is truly a gentle giant and the best butler I've ever seen."

"Does Christian always keep such a close acquaintance with his men?" Charlotte asked.

"That's why he opened this club. To help all the veterans he could." Alice went down a hall that ended with an entrance into a long room. "He cares so deeply, you see. He would help every veteran in England if he could."

Charlotte had no doubt of that. She followed Alice into the room and noted the long tables set out with chairs at regular intervals. Christian and Edward were just coming out of the kitchen.

Christian reached the ladies first and took Alice's arm and drew it through his. "I'm so glad you've arrived. It's nearly time."

"We stopped to talk to Reams," she said, smiling up at her husband. "Delilah is thriving in Surrey."

"Glad to hear it." He playfully touched the end of her nose. "Were you able to speak to your father today?"

"Not yet. I thought we'd stop at Huntingdon House on our way home." Alice leaned in.

Edward turned away from Alice and Christian and drew her to his side. He looked her over closely. "Are you well? You seem . . . different."

Charlotte wanted to throw her arms around him, feeling like she'd won back a small part of herself and needed to share that triumph, but she refrained since they were in public. Perhaps later, when they were at home.

"I'm quite well, thank you. I've really enjoyed Lady Alice's company. And the club is brilliant." She looked around at the men who were starting to come into the room.

An older woman wearing an apron approached them. "We're ready, Captain."

Christian nodded. "Thank you, Gemma. I've brought some helpers with me today."

Gemma looked shyly at Charlotte, then spoke to Alice. "Welcome. I'll find you aprons so you don't ruin your fine clothing, my lady."

"That would be lovely," Alice said. "And please, I hope you'll call me Alice. There shouldn't be any titles in here, don't you agree?"

Gemma's eyes went wide. "Oh, I don't know if I could do that, my la . . ." She stopped and glanced at Alice's raised eyebrows and expectant look, before revising what she was going to say. "If you wish me to . . . Alice."

"See, that wasn't so hard." Alice linked her arm with Gemma's. "I can hardly countenance how kind you're being since I'm the one who is intruding on your kitchen. Did your husband serve in the army?"

"Yes, he did . . . Alice." Gemma gave her a hesitant smile.

The rest of them followed Gemma and Alice back to the kitchen, listening to them chat about Gemma's husband who had died fighting in France. Charlotte was amazed at Alice's ability to befriend a new acquaintance so quickly, and to once again see how sincere she was in her offer of friendship. Gemma gave Charlotte an apron, which she put on, while taking in the tidy room. There were large pots of soup simmering and several loaves of bread cooling on a counter. "It smells wonderful."

"It's nothing fancy," Gemma said to Charlotte as she stirred one of the pots. "Just good food for the belly."

For the next hour Christian, Alice, Charlotte, and Edward served soup and bread to the former soldiers. Charlotte was nervous at first, since she'd never served anything more than tea, but she soon relaxed. The men were grateful and thanked her several times. It felt good to serve them in a small way. Edward had glanced her direction more than once. He had a new light in his eyes that warmed her every time she saw it. He was conquering his fears, just as she was conquering hers. And they'd be a better couple for it, too. She just knew it.

Charlotte did notice Edward looking closely into each man's face, but there was no sign of Marcus. It was disappointing, of course, but Edward wouldn't give up looking for him. Neither would she.

When the meal was over, Christian called for the carriage. "I'll keep watching for him," Christian told Edward as they made their way to the front door. "He'll turn up."

But Edward was focused on a man who was slumped on the floor in the far corner of the dining room with a dirty bandage wrapped around his forehead. Charlotte stepped closer.

Was it? It couldn't be.

But when Edward brushed past Christian and walked toward the man, Charlotte knew it was. She covered her mouth with her hand as she watched her husband kneel in front of the wounded man and look into his face.

"Marcus?" His voice choked on the words. "It's me, Edward."

CHAPTER 19

*E*dward walked into the townhouse with Marcus in his arms. He set him down on the chaise longue and stepped back.

"I can hardly believe he's here," Edward said, unable to quite tell if he was out of breath from exertion or excitement. He glanced at Charlotte, who looked as surprised as he felt. "It's like a wonderful dream."

"I'm so happy he's found." Charlotte stared at the man lying so still in front of them and Edward's gaze followed. Marcus was gaunt, his arms thin. Fabric was pinned to his trousers on one side where his lower left leg would have been. His hair and beard were long and shaggy. It was hard to tell anything about the man other than he needed a bath.

Marcus opened his eyes and stared, furrowing his brow as if he didn't know exactly where he was. He curled up his arms, as if he was cold, perusing the room before stopping to rest on Charlotte. She glanced at Edward and stepped forward.

Marcus wet his lips and visibly swallowed. "Charlie?" he rasped.

Tears rose in Edward's throat at the familiar endearment coming from his old friend. He would know that voice anywhere. It really was Marcus.

Charlotte knelt down on the carpet next to the chaise longue, staying close to his side. She carefully took his hand. "I'm here, Marcus."

His lips curved in a smile, but he closed his eyes as if being in the company of his friends was too much to take in all at once. "Forgive me for not standing."

Charlotte wiped the tears from her cheeks, and Edward was fighting back his own emotions.

"All is forgiven. You've returned to us." She *tsked* and shook her head. "You had us all in our blacks, mourning your death, you naughty man."

He opened his eyes again, but the light that had been there earlier was now extinguished. He turned his face away from her. "I should have stayed away, but I wanted to die on English soil. See the country I fought for one last time."

Edward drew his eyebrows down. Was Marcus dying? They needed a physician to look at him immediately, someone more than an exhausted surgeon trying to treat hundreds of men after a battle.

Charlotte didn't seem upset by Marcus's words. She continued to speak in low, soothing tones.

Edward was distracted when Christian entered and went to the doorway to confer with him. "Is the doctor on his way?"

"Yes, he'll be here momentarily." Christian looked over at Marcus and Charlotte. "Has he said much?"

"He recognized Charlotte." With the bandage around his head, Edward had been concerned that Marcus had suffered a head injury and perhaps wouldn't have his memory intact. But that didn't seem to be the case.

Edward turned back and rejoined Charlotte. Now that he knew the doctor was coming, he could focus on Marcus.

Christian followed on Edward's heels and stopped near Marcus's side. "Glad to be in your company again, Mr. Harper," Christian said. "We've been worried about you."

Marcus motioned to his one remaining leg. "I'm no use to anyone anymore, Captain. Just a cripple now."

His eyes were so bleak, the hollowness in his voice hinting at the mental and physical anguish he'd endured. The sound pained Edward to his core.

"We'll talk more of that when you're restored to health." Christian clasped his hands behind his back as if he wanted to say more, but thought the better of it. He retreated to a spot near the fireplace.

Charlotte patted Marcus's hand. "I need to send for some beef tea. Good English food will set you to rights in no time."

She stood next to Edward, all eyes in the room on Marcus. He shifted uncomfortably, not meeting their gazes.

"The doctor will be here momentarily. I'd like to move you to a bedchamber where you can bathe and change into fresh clothing," Edward said, breaking the silence.

"Ashamed of me already?" Marcus asked. His voice had an edge to it that Edward had never heard before.

"Of course not." Edward frowned. "You will rest easier if you're clean and fed. At least that's what my nanny always told me when I was in the sickroom."

"I'm not sick," Marcus said with a deep sigh. "I no longer have one of my legs. There isn't anything a doctor can do about that." He turned his face away. "If you could just find me an inn for a night or two, I'll be on my way."

Edward glanced at Charlotte, finding it difficult to hide his pain at Marcus's declaration. What could he say to comfort his old friend?

She set her hand on Edward's arm. "I'd love to have you as our first houseguest, Marcus," she said calmly. "My mother would never forgive me if we sent away a dear friend when you'd only just returned home. You know how strict she is about doing what's right and proper."

A ghost of a smile whispered across Marcus's lips. "She is a dragon about propriety."

"Then it's settled." She looked up at Edward. "Let's take him upstairs to the yellow room. It has a beautiful view of the back garden."

Edward gave her a grateful smile. Marcus didn't respond, merely nodded. She was brilliant. "Send the doctor upstairs when he arrives." Edward leaned in and gave her a quick kiss on the cheek. "And thank you," he whispered.

Bending he picked up Marcus and headed upstairs. Marcus was stiff in his arms and light as a child. Edward was alarmed at how he'd wasted away. They'd once been of similar stature. Guilt started to eat away at him again that he should have done more to save Marcus and spare him this, but he pushed the feelings back. That path had only led him to alcohol and he was finished with that.

Edward settled him on the bed, unable to keep his eyes off of Marcus. Beneath the beard and long hair, his best and oldest friend had returned from the dead. He really was alive

Only, he didn't seem as happy about that fact. Marcus glared at him, his eyes dark and angry. He turned away. "Stop staring. Just let me leave."

"Where would you go?" Edward sat on the bed, wanting to

reach out and hug him---prove that he was truly here in the flesh. But right now, that would not be well-received.

"I'll find a place." Marcus's voice was raspy, as if it had long been in disuse. What had he been through? Would he ever confide in Edward?

"I can't let you do that." Edward leaned forward, eager to talk to his friend, to have some semblance of the camaraderie they'd shared before. Marcus knew everything about him. They'd been closer than brothers. Surely that feeling between them hadn't disappeared and something of it still existed. Edward was afraid it might have, though, and swallowed hard at the thought.

Marcus tried to look around the room, but winced in pain. "Why did you bring me here?"

"You belong here. With me. With us. It seemed the natural thing to do." At Marcus's long, drawn-out sigh, as if being here was the last thing he wanted, Edward got up to pace. "I watched you die in that church along with a hundred other men. What happened? How did you survive?"

Marcus closed his eyes, whether because he was tired or didn't want to talk about his ordeal, Edward couldn't tell. But then Marcus spoke. "I nearly did die. After you and the regiment left, some Spanish women came to clear away the bodies. One realized I wasn't quite dead. She got her son and husband to bring me to their home. They nursed me back to health."

Edward's hands balled into fists. Wolverton had come through with orders to march on to the next town and be ready to meet the French on another battlefield. It had been a never-ending round. Only that day, they hadn't been able to bury their dead. They hadn't the time. It was the hardest thing Edward had ever done, leaving Marcus's body behind on a pew in that church. How had he not realized that Marcus was still alive? "I should have known. Made doubly sure you were gone before I marched out."

"You were under orders." Marcus shrugged. "From what I understood with my limited Spanish, my heartbeat was faint, and I was a breath away from death. I was unconscious for a very long time. I'm told the woman who took care of me wasn't sure I would ever wake. My wounds had festered. The village doctor couldn't do anything besides amputate my leg. So, when I had finally gained my senses, I was without a limb." Marcus looked down at the blankets that covered his stump. "I wished they had let me die."

"Because you didn't have your leg?" Edward sat in the chair again, trying to understand. "Losing you was the worst thing to ever happen to me. I'd let everyone down---you, your father, myself. I was supposed to protect you, and I failed." Edward folded his arms. "Why did you not send word to us?"

"I thought it better to let you go on thinking I'd died that day. I'm a cripple, of no use to anyone now." Marcus turned his face away.

Edward was dumbfounded. "Because you'd been wounded, you let your father . . . you let *me* . . . believe you were dead?"

When Marcus didn't answer, fury surged through Edward. "Do you know what that did to us? You are more than a blasted leg," Edward nearly shouted. "You're still here. Still you."

Marcus levered himself up to his elbows, his face flushed with anger. "What can I offer anyone besides being a lifelong burden? I can't make a living to ever support a wife and family. All I can do is sit and waste away."

"That's not true. I've heard of strides being made on wooden legs. Lord Anglesey was wounded at Waterloo, and his leg was amputated. He had a fine wooden one made and is said to move about quite well." Edward clutched the arms of his chair. He had to make Marcus see that there was hope yet. He was more than a cripple.

"I don't have enough blunt for that and even a wooden leg

wouldn't help me find a way to earn a living." Marcus lay flat again, frowning. "And I won't live off someone else's charity."

"I'd gladly pay for a wooden leg." Edward stared down at his old friend. "It's not charity, either. Marcus, you're like a brother to me. No one in the world knows me as well---except David and Charlotte."

"Have you married her, then?" There was an edge of harshness in Marcus's tone which flooded Edward with guilt. How was he allowed to be married and create a life while Marcus thought his was over?

"We married last week, actually." Edward thought of Charlotte's tender care and how she was the one who had given him his hope back. Maybe he could do that for Marcus. "She's quite anxious about you as well."

"The Spanish woman who took care of me reminded me of Charlotte sometimes. She was very efficient and seemed to know what I needed before anyone voiced it." Marcus closed his eyes. "When the French soldiers came to the house, she tried her best to hide me and cried when they took me away."

"What happened to her and her household?" Edward had to ask, but he didn't want to know. "Were they killed?"

"Thankfully, no. The French seemed happy to have another prisoner to add to their collection. They were most put out when they realized I had only one leg. They didn't want to carry me, so they left me with a lieutenant who lived just outside of the garrison." His hands rubbed over the counterpane, as if recalling the memory upset him. "He was half-English and disillusioned with the war. Talked endlessly of England. Made me homesick. It wasn't hard to convince him to bring me home, so he could find his relatives here."

Marcus's voice was sounding weaker. Edward should let him

rest, but he wanted to hear it all---and to tell Marcus what he'd done.

"I sent a message to your father to join us here the moment we found you." Edward made the statement quietly, knowing Marcus probably wouldn't like it.

"I wish you hadn't done that. I'm not ready." Marcus turned pain-filled eyes to Edward. "He won't want a cripple for a son."

Edward took his hand. "Marcus, he's mourned his only child. To have you back will seem a miracle. He won't give two figs about your leg."

A tear escaped Marcus's eye. "My father loves nothing more than putting in a full day's work."

"Yes, he's always taken pride in his work, but he loves you more than any of that." He squeezed Marcus's forearm. "How could you ever think you wouldn't be wanted or loved because you were wounded in battle?"

"I'd think you, of all people, could understand that. But you came back whole, so maybe I was mistaken, and you can't understand." Marcus pulled his arm away, bitterness seeping into his tone.

The words stung, but Edward wanted to make him see. "I might have come back physically whole, but not on the inside. I can't hear a thunderstorm without wanting to cower under a desk. I've used alcohol to numb myself so I can sleep without hearing men screaming in my nightmares or seeing you dying in my arms. I wake thrashing, and fear for anyone who comes into the room. All wounds can't be seen. Or healed."

Marcus searched Edward's eyes, seeing the pain reflected in his own. "You make me ashamed for my self-pity. I'm sorry, my brother."

"As am I." Edward reached for Marcus's arm, grateful he had the chance to ask forgiveness. To have a second chance with his friend. He'd longed for that opportunity so many times since the moment he'd left him behind.

"I've thought about you every day," Marcus said. "It just seemed so strange not having you with me. You made the army bearable. I've missed you terribly." He rolled to his side and threw his arms awkwardly around Edward. "I'm sorry. I'm so very sorry."

They both let their tears flow, purging all the guilt and anguish of the last months. Edward held his friend, finally able to put away the memory of holding him when he was dying and replacing that image with the one now of holding him, knowing he was going to live.

Edward reluctantly pulled away and stood to retrieve some handkerchiefs. When he returned, Edward mopped his face as Marcus did the same.

It was hard to put into words, but looking at Marcus, Edward felt as if the weight of the heavy burden of guilt he'd long carried had lifted off his shoulders. "I'm so glad you're here."

Marcus smiled for the first time since Edward had seen him in the club. "Me, too."

There was a knock at the door, and Charlotte peeked her head in. "I thought I heard voices. I have a tray of beef tea for our patient."

Edward nodded, and she came fully into the room, settling the tray on the table next to the bed. "Are you hungry?" she asked, looking into Marcus's face.

"Yes." He took her hand and pulled her closer to him. Clearing his throat, he offered his congratulations. "I was so pleased to hear you'd finally married Edward. Though I never saw what you liked about the chap, I know you had your heart set on him."

She squeezed Marcus's shoulder and grinned. "Yes, sometimes I had a difficult time seeing his good points, as well."

"Really, now, you two." Edward shook his head in mock-offense at the two of them. "We all know my handsome face turned Charlotte's head, and Marcus was just jealous when she didn't give him a second glance."

Charlotte chuckled and put her finger on her chin as if deep in thought. "Do you recall the day I fell in the mud trying to climb the stile after you and Marcus? Then you came back for me. You could have kept going and left me behind, but you were so gallant and even offered your handkerchief so I could wipe the mud off my cheek. I knew then you were the man I wanted to marry."

Marcus groaned and rolled his eyes. "He's always the hero." They all laughed at his downturned lips and exaggerated sad expression.

Edward remembered that day that she spoke of well. Charlotte was so doggedly determined to do exactly as he and Marcus did, they'd purposefully done things they knew she couldn't do well in a dress. He'd felt awful when she'd fallen. Her trusting, muddy face looking up at him was the moment he'd lost a bit of his heart to her.

He shifted closer, wanting to be near her. "I would have thought it was all those times I helped you rescue dogs, cats, birds, even hedgehogs. I was in Mrs. Blackhurst's black books for ages." Edward raised a brow. He'd also seen how tender Charlotte was during all those rescues and had lost another piece of his heart to her. It hadn't taken long before she'd owned his heart completely.

"Mrs. Blackhurst secretly loved our rescue adventures," Charlotte assured him with an airy wave of her hand. She looked to Marcus. "Regardless, nothing has been the same without you, Marcus. I'm so glad you're home."

Marcus watched them with a small smile on his face. At the sight of it, Edward suddenly felt in charity with all the world. Everything was as it should be.

Charlotte bent and kissed his cheek. Marcus flushed, but

smiled. "It's good to be home, though it's taken a while for me to get here," he told her. "I never thought I would miss beef tea."

"Is that a hint that you'd like some?" Charlotte helped him arrange the pillows behind his back so he could sit up and enjoy his tea. Before long, they were laughing at more memories they'd shared, and it seemed as if no time had passed at all since they'd parted.

Edward leaned back in his chair. He'd lived in darkness for so long, it was as if the sun had broken through the clouds and shone directly on him. He had his best friend back. He'd married the woman he loved.

Only two things remained to be done. He had to make peace with his father. And have the talk with his mother he'd been dreading.

But now he had the strength to do it.

CHAPTER 20

*C*harlotte arose early to prepare for Marcus's father's arrival. She dressed in her best day dress and had Millie put her hair in a tight chignon before she went down to the breakfast room. Cook had laid out a nice assortment of kippers, ham, poached eggs, toast, and tea on the sideboard and Charlotte took a little of each dish. Edward joined her just as she was finishing her meal. He looked adorably rumpled, though he couldn't have had a comfortable rest.

"Did you sleep in a chair by his bed all night?" she asked solicitously.

"Yes. I didn't want to leave him alone. Half of me was afraid he would try to leave, and the other half wanted to make sure he wasn't a dream." Edward sat down and poured himself a cup of tea.

Charlotte rose and filled a plate for him with a little of everything from the sideboard. He really did look exhausted. She placed it in front of him, hoping the food would restore some of his energy.

"Thank you," he said, poking the food with a fork. "You're up early." He yawned and blinked at the sunlight coming through the window.

"I assume Mr. Harper will be here early, and I wanted to be ready for him. I had the maids air out a room close to Marcus." Charlotte took another sip of her tea. "Perhaps I should have had that room made up for you."

"Once his father arrives, I'm sure I won't be needed." Edward picked up a piece of toast and put his favorite orange marmalade on it. He chewed slowly, as if trying to think of something to say. "Marcus slept most of the night and didn't seem to be in too much pain. I hope his mood will have improved when he awakens."

"He's been through so much. I'm sure he just needs time." Charlotte finished her tea. "I'll have Cook fix a tray for him."

Before she could rise, Lambson appeared at the door. "Mr. Harper has arrived, my lord, and the dowager viscountess. They are awaiting you in the parlor."

The dowager viscountess? Charlotte hadn't been expecting Edward's mother, but it was a pleasant surprise. She would have to alert the housekeeper.

"Very good." Edward stood and wiped his mouth with a serviette, then quickly brushed any breadcrumbs from his lap. He strode to the door and Charlotte followed close behind. He turned to take her hand, and Charlotte smiled at his thoughtfulness. She wanted to be with him, and it made her feel good that he wanted her with him, too.

When they entered the parlor, Mr. Harper was pacing in front of the fireplace and Edward's mother was sitting in a chair near the window, silently watching him.

Mr. Harper whirled around at their arrival. "Is it true?" he said, striding to Edward. "He's alive?"

Edward touched the old steward's shoulder, his voice shaking with the happiness and emotion of the news. "Yes. It's true. He's here."

Mr. Harper lifted his hand to his mouth to stifle a sob. "I must see him."

"He's upstairs. But, I must warn you, sir, he's not himself." Edward was hesitant to give him the rest of the news, that much was clear. "He's . . . he's lost a leg."

Mr. Harper didn't even blink when he heard. "Can I go to him?" He was obviously ready to start searching the house to find his son immediately.

"Of course." Edward reached for Charlotte. "Right this way. Oh, and Mother, will you ring for a tea tray? I shan't be long."

"Yes, don't worry about me," she told him as she settled in her chair and folded her hands in her lap.

Leading the way out of the parlor and up the stairs, Charlotte could feel Edward's anxiety as they walked down the hall. How would Marcus's father react to seeing his wounded son? Would this meeting be as Marcus feared?

Edward knocked and entered the room without waiting for a reply. "Marcus," he said quietly. "You have a visitor."

Marcus looked quite different than the last time Charlotte had seen him. His hair was combed and he was clean-shaven. He had been given a nightshirt and Edward's best banyan to wear. She was surprised to see him sitting up in bed with a cup of tea in his hand. He looked much more like the man she remembered.

When Marcus saw his father, he put the teacup down and straightened as if he were about to be scolded. "Father."

Mr. Harper went to his son's bedside and sat next to him. He cradled his son's face in his hands, his shoulders shaking with emotion. "My son, my son," he murmured over and over. "I thought I'd lost you." He bent over and laid his head on Marcus's chest.

Marcus stroked his father's hair as if he were the parent and his father the child. "Shh, don't take on so."

His father sat up to look into his son's face, the shock still evident in his eyes. "Having you returned to me is the greatest gift I've ever received. I've sat alone, night after night, remembering your mother, remembering you, and cursing God that I was old, without any living family. I wanted to die so I could join you both. And then God returned you to me." He pulled Marcus to him and held him close. "I love you. Oh, how I love you."

Marcus's tears streamed down his face, and he could barely choke out any words. "I've lost my leg, Father. The infection was too much. They couldn't save it."

Mr. Harper didn't even look down at the empty spot in the bedclothes where his son's left leg should have been. "You're here. Alive. That's all that matters."

"I'm sorry. I'm so sorry. I thought you wouldn't want a son without a leg. That's why I stayed away and let you think I was dead." Marcus was weeping openly. "I'm so sorry that I caused you so much pain."

The men cried in each other's arms, and Charlotte could no longer hold back her own tears. Edward quietly pulled her toward the door, and they left Marcus and his father alone.

They stood in the hall for a moment, not saying anything. Then Edward reached for her, and she went into his arms. She wept openly onto his shirtfront as he held her. His arms seemed to absorb all the grief and pain, the joy and happiness of the moment—all the emotions they'd had and held in the past few weeks.

Edward took out his handkerchief and dabbed at her tears. "I never could bear to see you cry," he said softly.

"I've always hated to cry in front of you. I wanted you to think me as brave as you were." She held his hand in hers and smiled at all the memories between them. "But seeing Marcus reunited with his father was worth the tears."

"I agree, but you must believe you have always been the bravest woman I've ever known." He stroked her cheek, his touch petal-soft, yet the warmth of his fingers sent a wave of heat through her frame. "You give me courage as well."

She leaned her cheek into his palm and put her hands on his chest, her heart drumming an accelerated rhythm at being so close to him. Her gaze strayed to his lips and she closed her eyes, wishing they had a few more moments alone. With a sigh, she opened them.

"Your mother is waiting for you. Though I did notice you seemed a bit anxious when she arrived. Did you need some courage to face her?" she teased.

"I sent for her." Edward slid his hands to her shoulders, loosely holding her in place, keeping her close. "It's time I truly lay my father's ghost to rest for good."

Charlotte's arms went around him, enjoying the circle of his embrace around her shoulders. "Do you want me to go down with you? Or should I retire to my room?"

"Come with me. It will be easier for me with you there." Edward kissed the top of her head. "If you want to."

"There's nowhere I'd rather be." She hugged him to her before they moved apart, though she kept close to his side. Taking his arm, they walked down the stairs to the parlor where Edward's mother was waiting patiently. A tray had been brought in with some of the breakfast selection, and she was just finishing her egg.

"How is Mr. Harper? He was as white as parchment the whole trip here and barely able to say a word. It was such a shock to get your message. What a joyful miracle it is for all of us." His mother used the serviette to dab at her mouth as she waited for Edward's reply.

"He's as well as can be expected." Edward seated Charlotte on the sofa and sat beside her. "We're giving him a few moments alone with Marcus."

His mother watched him, a knowing look in her eye. "And after seeing Marcus with his father, you'd like to talk about yours?"

Edward shifted closer to Charlotte and took her hand in his. Talking about his father had always been difficult. She leaned into him to give him silent support.

"Did you read the letter he left for you, Edward?" His mother's words were soft. She shook her head "No, I suppose you didn't or I wouldn't be here."

She sighed and moved forward in her chair, her face earnest, as if she wanted Edward to really hear what she was about to say. "You leaving and joining the army were like a clarion call to your father. It was as if he'd awoken and realized how he'd mishandled your upbringing. He regretted so many things about how you'd been raised. He wanted to call his words back. He went over and over your last argument and wished he could do things differently. Tell you he loved you. But the chance was gone. He didn't give himself the excuse that he'd raised you exactly as his father had raised him—respecting duty and responsibility because that's what set you apart as a true gentleman. He thought he was doing what was best for you and realized too late he was wrong." His mother let out a long breath as if saying those things had taken all of her strength.

"I have a hard time imagining Father regretting anything. He was so set in his ways." Edward's voice was low, but steady.

"I know. But I was a witness to his remorse. He did all he could to get word of you while you were in Spain. He got reports from your commanding officers and offered to buy you higher commissions. He was angry when you turned them down—angry and proud at the same time. You were making your own way as a man, in ways he'd never imagined. He wanted to tell you so before he passed, but he understood why you didn't come to him." His mother took out her handkerchief to wipe her tears away. "Your father and I were not a love match, you know, but I grew to respect him, especially in the last year of his life. He changed, Edward."

Edward rose and kneeled in front of his mother, taking her small hand in his. "I'm sorry I didn't come. I wish *I* could go back."

She smiled and patted his cheek. "Sometimes I do see your father in you. But I fear he did you a great disservice, my son. He instilled in you the attributes of duty and responsibility to the point where you felt an overwhelming sense of it for those around you—one that no man could ever live up to. You can't be responsible for the choices of others. No matter how much you love them."

Charlotte could feel the tears pricking the back of her throat. His mother's words made so much sense now that she knew how horribly Edward had suffered when he thought Marcus had died.

His mother went on. "I want you to know that forgiveness is a strength, too, and forgiving yourself is essential. Your father loved you in his way and wanted your forgiveness. I hope knowing about your father's change of heart will help you as you begin your new life." She dabbed at her eyes again. "He wrote it all in his letter to you, in his own words."

He kissed her hand. "Thank you, Mother, for being so patient with me as I muddled through all of this. I'd like to come home for the holidays as we planned and get reacquainted."

"I would be delighted." She stood, and Edward stood with her. They reached for Charlotte, and the three of them made a small circle. "I'm so proud of both of you. I've watched you find your way back to each other as you've overcome so many obstacles. I always wanted to see you married and happy, and I'm so glad I got my wish."

She put her arms around them and squeezed. "Now I'm going to go upstairs to lie down and try to recover myself from the mad dash we made to London this morning." They stepped back and she put her palm on Edward's shoulder. "I love you, my son. Never doubt that."

He leaned down to kiss her cheek. "And I love you, Mother."

She pressed her handkerchief over her heart. "I'll see you at dinner this evening. Though, if you or Mr. Harper need anything, you can come for me."

"Yes, Mother."

Charlotte watched him escort his mother to the hallway, then sank down onto the sofa. What an emotional day it had been already—and it wasn't even noon! Edward came back into the room and joined her.

"I'm so overwhelmed," he said, tucking her against his side and letting his hand slide over her shoulder.

"In a good way?" she asked snuggling closer. His eyes were weary, but a new light was in them that spoke of the peace he was working to claim.

"Yes, though I wish I hadn't let pride rob me of so many things. Reconciliation with my father. Asking for help in overcoming my difficulties. Hurting you." He paused and exhaled. "I never want to hurt you again, Charlotte. I love you. I've loved you for as long as I can remember."

She turned in his arms and reached up to touch his jaw, his stubble scraping her fingers. What a wifely thing to feel. "I love you, too, Edward. You've owned my heart since I was a girl."

He bent down and touched his lips to hers. She closed her eyes and reveled in the feelings he evoked in her. Warmth had started in her middle and was spreading throughout her body. His hand went to the nape of her neck while his other held her close to his chest. The kiss deepened, and Charlotte didn't want him to stop. She'd never felt anything like this before, as if all of the love she felt for him was wrapped up in one kiss.

He pulled back slightly and pressed his forehead to hers. "I'm the luckiest man in England."

She chuckled, barely able to catch her breath. "Only England? I've got my work cut out for me, then." And she tilted her chin up and kissed him again.

CHAPTER 21

*E*dward felt like a new man. He had his beautiful wife on his arm and they were about to be announced at the Wolverton ball. Though attending a ball wasn't in the strictest of propriety after only six months of mourning, it was still in bounds. Edward hadn't wanted to turn down the invitation since this would be their first ball as a married couple.

"Are you nervous?" he asked, bringing Charlotte's hand to his mouth and pressing a kiss to the back of it. He didn't even glance behind him to see if he'd shocked anyone by kissing his wife's hand in public.

"A little." She smoothed her skirts again and took a deep breath. "The last time I was at a ball was so . . . difficult."

He hated seeing any insecurity on her face and hastened to reassure her. "You're a different woman now. You've faced down your dragons. And, should you need any assistance, I'll help you be brave. Or, perhaps we should shock all of society right where we stand and start some new rumors." He waggled his eyebrows suggestively, and moved closer to lean down for a quick kiss on her lips. She smiled, and some of the tenseness seemed to leave her shoulders.

Edward was sorely tempted to kiss her again, but if he did so, he might forget himself and muss the coiffure her maid had worked hard to make just right. "You know, I may need you to help *me* be brave. I haven't danced at a ball in a very long time. What if I've forgotten all the steps? Your toes could bear the brunt of my forgetfulness."

"I'm sure the steps will come back to you." She pressed into his arm and interlaced their fingers. "I wish we could dance every dance, but that wouldn't be seemly."

He raised his eyebrows. "Well, I do plan to steal you away to the gardens for an improper amount of time."

She laughed, and the sound warmed his heart. "What a rogue you are. I am fair warned."

When it was their turn to be announced, Charlotte was happy and relaxed, just as he'd hoped.

"The Viscount and Viscountess Carlisle."

The conversation buzzing throughout the room stopped and many guests turned to watch them enter. Edward could hardly take his eyes off Charlotte as he escorted her in. Her green dress accented her eyes and coloring. The Carlisle emeralds sparkled at her neck and ears. She was beautiful inside and out. And she was his wife.

He led her to the receiving line, where Christian and Alice were waiting to greet them as their host and hostess. After the customary greetings complete with bows and curtsies, Christian leaned in. "How is Marcus?"

Edward was happy to give a good report. "Better. He's using crutches now and plans to return home with his father in a few days."

It was hard to believe the change in Marcus in the few weeks since they'd found him. He'd been able to talk about his injury and months of recovery. The French lieutenant he'd been with had actually been a great help and comfort. Edward hoped to find and reward him if he could. Marcus still had a long recovery ahead, but he was well on his way and had so many people to support and love him.

"I'm glad to hear he's improving," Christian said. "We'd like to come and see him off, if that's amenable."

"Why don't you come for dinner tomorrow evening? I'm sure Marcus would love to see you," Charlotte told him. "And you might enjoy a quiet evening with friends after throwing the event of the season." She looked around at the crush of people.

Alice's eyes followed her gaze. "One thing I've always enjoyed doing is giving a ball. My mother is a master at planning and taught me well." She leaned toward Charlotte, conspiratorially. "Did you know, I met Christian at one of my mother's balls—and I have some fond memories of that introduction." She gave him a sly grin.

Christian inclined his head with a hint of merriment in his eyes. "Yes, that ball was quite memorable. Unforgettable, really."

They were obviously trying to hold back laughter, and the love between them was quite easy to see. Edward hoped that same sentiment could be said about him and Charlotte as well someday.

Alice turned to them, a faint blush pinking her cheeks at her husband's flirtations. "Forgive us. We'd be delighted to come for dinner tomorrow."

Edward looked at the line of people still waiting to be received by Christian and Alice. Their time was at an end. He bowed. "Until then."

Taking Charlotte's arm, he led her toward the dance floor. "Have I told you how beautiful you look tonight?" he asked as he put his other hand over hers resting on his forearm.

"Yes. Several times. But I can bear to hear it again." She pressed closer to his side. "Do you remember our first dance at the village Harvest Ball right after I turned sixteen? I could hardly breathe, you looked so dashing."

"You were a vision." He had hardly been able to keep his eyes off of her. It was the first time he'd realized how truly beautiful she was. He'd danced the allowed two sets with her and had wished for more all evening.

Charlotte smiled and shook her head. "You flatter me, sir. But I must say, you've outdone yourself tonight." She glanced at him from head to toe, and he stood straighter at her perusal. "Gibbs must have been so proud of the mathematical knot in your cravat. The diamond stickpin is understated, and yet perfect for your evening ensemble. *You* are a vision."

"You flatter me, madam."

They laughed at their shared jest, and for just a moment, the rest of the crowd faded away until Edward could see only her. Charlotte's smile and her presence next to him was the one thing he'd been sure he couldn't have—and definitely didn't deserve—when he'd returned to England. He was so very glad his life as a bachelor forever alone had never been realized. "I love you."

Her eyes widened at his unexpected declaration. "I love you, too," she said fervently. She bit her lip. "I would never want to be accused of being scandalous, but if we were alone, I would kiss you."

"I might enjoy a bit of scandal with you. Perhaps we can go to the garden for some air," Edward suggested, arching a brow. "No one would notice us missing."

"But the musicians are about to begin." She nodded toward the small dais where they were tuning their instruments. "We wouldn't want Christian and Alice to notice our absence, and they surely would, if we didn't dance the first set."

Just as she finished speaking, the music began. "A waltz." Edward drew close enough to speak softly in her ear. "My favorite."

The crowd parted, and Alice and Christian led out onto the dance floor. Edward squeezed Charlotte's hand. "I recall that I once promised to waltz with you at our wedding ball. While this is not exactly our wedding ball, I'd still like to dance that waltz. If you'll have me."

Her eyes were soft as she looked at him. "I'd be delighted."

They joined the other couples on the dance floor and got into position. Edward loved having her in his arms. As he drew her to him, he might have held her just a little too close for propriety's sake, but he didn't care. This was what they'd dreamed of all those years ago from that first dance at the Harvest Ball, to their plans of a grand wedding. He didn't want to forget a moment of this night.

"What are you thinking about?" she asked as they twirled close to the French doors leading to the gardens.

"Being alone with you." Her lilac scent teased his nose and his hand tightened on hers.

Her throaty laugh went right to his heart. "You are in a roguish mood tonight."

He let out a long-suffering sigh. "I'll try to remember my manners."

They finished the dance looking into each other's eyes as if this truly were a ball celebrating their union. He'd never been so happy.

When the set concluded, Edward led her to the lemonade table. Another lady was there waiting to be served, and Charlotte greeted her warmly. "Lady Elizabeth, how are you enjoying the ball?"

Lady Elizabeth gave her a faint smile and blushed deeply. "V-very well, my lady. Thank you."

"Lady Alice informed me that you are to come to the Veterans Club next week to help us serve the afternoon meal. I'm so delighted to be able to further our acquaintance." Charlotte accepted a cup of lemonade from Edward. "And may I make known to you my husband, Viscount Carlisle? My lord, this is my recent acquaintance, Lady Elizabeth, daughter of the Duke of Barrington."

Edward bowed. "A pleasure to meet you, my lady." He put his hand on Charlotte's back. "My wife has told me about your charity work with Lady Alice. Quite commendable."

Elizabeth curtsied. "Th-thank you, my lord." She blushed again. "I'm just f-fetching a drink for my mother. If you'll excuse me?" She bobbed a curtsy and carefully turned with a glass of lemonade in hand before she disappeared into the crowd.

Charlotte watched her go. "Lady Elizabeth is recently betrothed." She took a sip of her drink before continuing. "She's a little shy, but Alice speaks so highly of her. From the few words she's said to me, I hope to be friends. It's been so wonderful to meet other ladies who don't have a high opinion of Society gossip and truly care about others."

"She'd be lucky to have you for a friend." Edward took the glass and set it on the table, before clasping her hand and leading her to the French doors that led outside. "As I am. Shall we take a turn in the garden, my lady?"

Charlotte laughed as they strolled outside and headed to a secluded bench where the light from the ballroom gave way to shadows. Edward drew her close, his arm assuming its familiar position around her shoulders. "Are you happy, my love?"

"Deliriously." She snuggled into his side. "Are you?"

"Yes. Although I must say, I'm grateful that you don't mind me drinking gallons and gallons of tea and having the leather bag hung in one of the guest rooms for my pursuit of pugilism."

Removing all the alcohol from the house hadn't been extremely hard for Edward. Not having any to tempt him was just good sense. Now, during a storm, he retreated to the guest room to pummel the leather bag. Or he sought out Charlotte's company. And the intensity of his night terrors had lessened considerably since Marcus had returned. Having him home truly was a miracle on many counts.

Charlotte tilted her head to look at him but stayed in his arms. "I rather like how refreshed you feel after your sessions in the guest room. And drinking tea is quite healthy for you, I'm sure." Her eyes were bright with happiness and warmth radiated through Edward's chest. "I think you're nearly ready to challenge some of the men at the Veterans Club."

"Would you wager I would win?" he teased.

"Of course." She raised herself a little more so she could face him, a wide smile on her face. "I believe in you. But perhaps just a few more practice sessions are in order. Just to be sure."

"Oh, ho! Well, as my wife, I will take your advice." Edward gently nudged her chin upward until they were only a breath apart. His heartbeat was starting to kick up its rhythm at her nearness. "Before we were wed, you wanted to be courted properly, so we could get to know each other after being apart for so long. I know that circumstances prevented that, and while it's not quite conventional, I would be happy to court you now. I want to make all your wishes come true."

She lightly kissed him and drew back with a smile. "You already have. Many times over."

His hand cradled her head as he moved to capture her lips. He tenderly kissed her mouth, then trailed little kisses across her jaw to her ear. "I once vowed to find you after the war and make you mine. But you found me, Charlotte. You never gave up on me."

"And you were worth all my energy and effort," she whispered, wrapping her arms around his neck. "We were meant to be together."

His thumb traced over her bottom lip. "And I'll do all in my power to ensure that we'll be together for now and for always." That was one vow he'd never break.

And then he pressed his lips to hers again, sealing the sentiment with a kiss to remember.

Don't miss the next book in the series, **The Highlander's Hidden Heart.**

A duke's daughter. A Highland warrior. And a love worth fighting for.

Lady Elizabeth has done her best to secure an advantageous match, but a shy nature, combined with a stutter, hasn't helped her cause. After two Seasons, her father won't wait any longer and promises her to a man she despises. There doesn't seem to be anything Elizabeth can do beyond wish for a freedom she'll never have---until a charming Highlander appears.

Alec Ramsay unexpectedly inherits an earldom and must leave his beloved Scottish Highlands to present himself in London and settle the estate affairs. After meeting his new neighbor, Lady Elizabeth, he feels a connection to her that he's never felt with any other woman. Alec makes every effort to further their acquaintance, but soon finds out that Elizabeth could be swept out of his reach before they have a chance to explore the feelings between them. With everything at stake, can he risk all for a chance at love?

Did you miss the first book in the series?

Lord Christian Wolverton—known as Wolf in a covert group operating during the war against Napoleon—has been called home from his military duties. However, information falls into his hands that a traitor will soon try to tip the scales back into French favor and Christian doesn't have much time to stop it from happening.

Going to the powerful Duke of Huntingdon for help, Christian comes face to face with Lady Alice. She's a beautiful member of the ton with a very big secret—she's also a trained agent and already on the case. Forced to partner with her to lure the traitor out of hiding, Christian wants to quickly close the case himself, before Lady Alice is more closely involved. But Lady Alice has ideas of her own and she's going to prove her theories correct—with or without him.

Danger is closer than they think, however, and it's a race against time to expose the traitor's identity before British lives are endangered. Both Christian and Alice have strong opinions on who he is, but which one will be proven right?

Julie Coulter Bellon is an award-winning author of nearly two dozen published books. Her book The Marquess Meets His Match won a five star review from Readers' Favorite, All Fall Down won the RONE award for Best Suspense, Pocket Full of Posies won a RONE Honorable Mention for Best Suspense and The Captain was a RONE award finalist for Best Suspense. Most recently her books, The Capture and Second Look were both Whitney finalists for Best Suspense/Mystery.

Julie loves to travel and her favorite cities she's visited so far are probably Athens, Paris, Ottawa, and London. In her free time, she loves to read, write, teach, watch Hawaii Five-O, and eat Canadian chocolate. Not necessarily in that order.

If you'd like to be the first to hear about Julie's new projects and receive a free book, you can sign up to be part of her VIP group on her website www.juliebellon.com

facebook.com/AuthorJulieCoulterBellon
twitter.com/juliebellon
instagram.com/AuthorJulieCoulterBellon